LADY V.
and other stories

D. R. POPA

*Julietei d' lui Cori —
prieteni de rară calite
sufletească, minunat
nebuni replantiți ca
și mine în lumea Nouă —
cu vechea d' stabra*

dragoste

6/28/09

*du noștra
Peligrad*

SPUYTEN DUYVIL
New York City

"*Lady V.*" and "*The Choice*" have been translated into English by Simina Calin. "*Panic Syndrome!*" has been translated by Calin-Andrei Mihailescu and Ramona Uricescu, and first published in "*Exquisite Corpse*". The Latin translations into English in "*The Choice*" have been graciously done by Liana Lupas, PhD. Thanks for Carmen Firan's support and literary solidarity. Special thanks to Jean Harris who was the first reader (and advisor) of this book. My good old friend Calin-Andrei Mihailescu applied the last touches on the manuscript. All my gratitude to him. The cover: James Abbott McNeill Whistler. Rose and Silver: The Princess from the Land of Porcelain. 1864. Oil on canvas. Used her by permission from the Freer Gallery of Art, Washington, DC

Library of Congress Cataloging-in-Publication Data

Popa, Dumitru Radu.
[Selections. English]
Lady V., and other stories / D.R. Popa.
p. cm.
Includes bibliographical references and index.
ISBN-13: 978-1-933132-31-0 (alk. paper)
I. Title.

PC840.26.O5278A2 2006
859'.134--dc22
2006022048

Printed in Canada

LADY V. and other stories

LADY V.

S o that, after four—oh so tumultuous!—marriages, Mrs. V. managed to escape with her virginity intact, and, God knows!, anyone could tell that this was none of her doing. At an age when other women begin to wilt, or begin to show those unmistakable signs of old age—puckers at the corners of their eyes, their mouth hardened, shoulders slightly stooped, their walk pinched or heavy depending on their build, but most of all the extinguished spark in their gaze, sometimes absolutely devastating in its desperation—all of these I have seen so many times!—none of them could be found in Mrs. V.'s face. And, it seems, she was to maintain that same charm, that same ageless freshness and femininity, until well near her eightieth birthday (after the discovery of the journal it could be established with certainty that she had been born in 1917, not ten years later as most people guessed, probably because her physiognomy froze in time at a hard-to-place age—somewhere around forty?).

In all four cities where her marriages, about which enough has been said already, took her, she was known as Lady V. And strangely, this woman, who was to die a virgin, had always been seen as a *Lady*, ever since she was a child. Ever since her old *mamie* Jemmima, who had raised her in her parents' gigantic house in Georgia, had seen her—on one of those impossible afternoons when the thermometer rises above 100 degrees and the relative humidity is also almost 100—wiping the sweat off her forehead with an embroidered handkerchief. The act, for a girl of only five, seemed to her uncanny: the movements were utterly unrushed, her fingers, extremely long and extremely thin, barely pressed on the handkerchief; the whole thing had something Levantine about it, patient and clear, enchanting and noble, and when the girl placed the handkerchief on the little basalt table next to the armchair, only to take, with the same meticulousness and apparent disregard for the tedium of life, the purple fan that she then waved to the right and to the left, more as if she were performing a stylized dance than as if she was truly trying to cool off, Jemmima crossed herself and exclaimed: *Good Lord, that's a Lady!* There was, in fact, a hidden meaning behind this exclamation. The girl's mother could hardly be called a *lady*, and old Jemmima, who in her day had known some of the veritable Southern aristocracy used the term with a certain amount of reluctance to address that Northern carpetbagger who had gotten rich overnight by marrying an oil-man, one who was as much an *arriviste* as she was, and who now lived in one of the most attractive old residences in Atlanta.

But this child was, surely, something entirely different. From that day on, everyone, some more, some less seriously, called the little five-year-old girl *Lady Victory* and, not much later, *Lady V.*

*****

Victory Hapburn-Barnes was her full name, though, unfortunately, or who knows, perhaps fortunately, nothing glorious had happened in her life to justify it. Despite this, the unreal peace that her appearance lent to a room, her perfect grasp of good manners and her innocent, detached air could, I think, constitute a victory in and of itself. A victory probably more over the dizzying fragments—her life, divided among four disastrous marriages in four different grand cities—that would have destroyed anyone even a bit callous.

Neither *Hapburn* nor *Barnes* meant anything in Georgia (had she had been named Jackson like practically everyone else it wouldn't have made any difference!), but her parents' insistence on advertising a hyphenated name, and one which didn't even have any special significance, spoke volumes about the naked pretensions of a couple of Yankees who'd made their fortune in the South.

This, however, is of very little importance, even though Lady V.'s journal (found more or less through happenstance) clearly shows her wish to understand the Northerners' biting rejection, which sprung perhaps from the incompatibility of two mentalities difficult to bridge even after a century. Indeed, Lady V. herself had almost forgotten that her real name was Hapburn-Barnes just as she had not, somewhat unusually, taken any of her four husbands' names: McNeill, Kaplan, Villefort, or Rehnquist.

No one ever knew just how rich she was. In fact the luxurious apartment on Madison Avenue was of great value in and of itself, and then it's almost certain that the two houses, one near Glasgow and the other in an elegant section of London, had been perpetually rented and brought in a high enough income so that she did not feel compelled to touch her savings, the only tangible remnants of her four marriages. She had sold the house in Neuilly or so can be deduced from her diary. She could no longer stand the idea of owning something so close to Paris. She had loved the city frenetically and, after Michel Villefort's death, she abandoned France and left all the details of selling the house in the hands of a lawyer, who had no qualms about selling the property for a ludicrous price (actually he sold it to some of his wife's relatives whose descendents are still living there).

******

The four cities where Lady V. had been married, London, Paris, Glasgow and New York, are all proud possessors of excellent art collections. Each has, moreover, numerous paintings by Whistler, who lived and worked in each.

Lady V.'s passion for Whistler grew gradually. It began in her youth (if normal concepts of age apply to someone like her). She spent that part of her life in London as the very young fiancée of a banker. One day during that time, while she was at the Tate Gallery walking for the umpteenth time through the rooms, the invitation to her wedding with Gregor McNeill fell out of her purse. An excessively elegant gentleman—one could have called him *Le Comte de Montesquoiu*[1] if one were to stay within the register, both Whistlerian and Proustian, of that atmosphere—rushed to pick it up. He looked at her quickly but thoroughly from head to toe, then gave it back to her, obviously and intentionally touching her thin, cream leather glove. The gesture seemed a bit perverse, lasting much longer than necessary, and Lady V. imagined that it would never end, that, in that slow-motion movement, everything would be suspended somewhere outside of reality in the same state that haunted her from time to time and always left her with a light-headed, guilty, fainting feeling that she would have liked to shake off, but which she made no effort to either reject or let run to its inevitable conclusion....

"Congratulations," said the gentleman after Lady V. had her invitation back. "Well then, I see we'll soon be *Lady McNeill*!" he said with a somewhat mocking tone. "Any relation to the painter, I mean... in your husband's family?"

Although she had no desire to start a conversation with this person, she felt compelled to ask him: "What painter?"

The gentleman laughed loudly, somewhat disturbingly, and then looked at Lady V.'s face, looked past her at the painting, and after repeating this annoying exercise a few times, finally exclaimed: "Strange! I suppose it could be just a coincidence ... of some kind ... never mind your husband's family... but you, you yourself look shockingly like the girl in the picture ... you

[1] *Robert de Montesquiou-Fezensac* (1855-1921), aesthete, taste-maker, homosexual, aristocratic scion of France's oldest lineages.

were looking at her, weren't you? At any rate, I don't want to bother you … Truly shocking, there's no other word for it! Again, congratulations on your marriage!"

Lady V. felt dizzy, slightly so, then immediately the urge to leave the room as quickly as she could, and finally, the curiosity to look at the painting on the wall behind her. She didn't turn around all of a sudden, but very slowly and with her eyes closed. Even when she was facing the wall she didn't open her eyes. She took a few breaths, tried to imagine what could be in the painting; she did this many times with so many things, she practiced a kind of ritualistic approach to every instant, from the most banal to the most important. She couldn't imagine anything distinctly, so she slowly opened her fingers in front of her eyes, and the light filtered through bringing with it the portrait of a young girl—of uncertain age—wearing a white dress with a creamy, silk sash accentuating her high waist; her hair was thick and long, gathered in an ebony ornament. She wore a pair of embroidered slippers and held her feet like a ballerina; her left hand holding a dark green-brown hat looked unspeakably soft. As unspeakable for that matter was the background of the painting, with its gray and brown tones, its two unreal butterflies, and a few floating daisies, probably coming out of a vase just off the canvas.

All these things did in fact go very well with Mrs. V.'s *demeanor*, but someone would have needed a rich imagination, or truly ravishing powers of observation, to deduce from these odd and mostly atmospheric details a resemblance, not to mention a shocking one, to the painting, or rather, to the face of the girl painted there: fleshy lips, a well-defined nose with sensuous nostrils, large black eyes slightly too far apart under harshly arched eyebrows and a willful forehead.

Lady V. could not stop laughing, openly and with obvious relief, and those who were visiting the Tate Gallery at that early hour stopped to admire the enchanting sight of this young woman laughing so naturally in front of a painting.

Then, and ever after, Lady V. could not stand to be ridiculous, to find herself in an awkward situation like the ones that others were so willing to put up with: endless conversations about the weather, about the unpredictable twists of fashion, or frivolous discussions about the state of society and what should be done. How many times had she been part of these, and every time, more as a means of protecting herself so that she could *survive*, she had come up with a mantra that she repeated in her head without anyone realizing how troubled she was: *"I am not here, I am not here! This is not happening to me!"*

That morning at the Tate she recited her mantra before looking up at the painting again. She then read the short description on the plaque to the right: *Whistler (James McNeill): Harmony in Gray and Green. Miss Cicely Alexander (1872).* She took a few steps back, looked at the painting one more time. The notion that, in fact, the canvas represented not so much a portrait as a harmonious combination of colors delighted her enormously and she told herself that she would immediately and forever forget the name of Cicely Alexander, remembering instead only the atmosphere of the painting that so resembled her. In fact, Lady V. hadn't even seen a portrait there, but rather a room overarched by nuances and maybe finely mingled and hard to discern scents. She had the vague and calming sensation—one that she would have again quite often in the other major cities where her marriages took her while standing in front of Whistler's works—that she could clearly and quite easily step into the painting without disturbing any of the composition's harmony. Sometimes she gave in to this feeling, realizing that nothing extraordinary happened except that maybe for a few seconds she felt herself to be both watcher and watched. And from this point on, anything, or so she felt, could happen in these surroundings that she had never been in before but that, none the less, she recognized in great detail.

She felt suspended between space and time, but she could never determine the length or intensity of this strange feeling.

******

The young man examining the portrait on the easel wore a long, burgundy scarf wrapped around his neck and hanging nonchalantly, or perhaps with studied nonchalance, over his shoulder. He had run up the stairs, it was clear; he was breathing quickly. He walked towards the window that took up the entire wall facing the street. He hesitated, deciding between opening it—oh, the thought that he would immediately hear the unbearable rattle of carriages and the shouting of the newspaper peddlers!—or just pulling the drapes closed. He easily decided on the second, but the way he pulled at the curtain betrayed some annoyance or unease. He carelessly threw on his brown robe over his street clothes without buttoning it, picked up a brush biting its end from time to time, and stared intensely at himself in the mirror hanging to the left of the easel. He turned again to the self-portrait, bit his upper lip, almost invisible under the blonde mustache, turned the mirror, threw the brush on the floor, took his head in his hands and mumbled: "Perfect... couldn't be better... what select company! Sargent and Watts and Fildes should be well pleased ... It's just that being so limited they won't understand what is essential. As a matter of fact, I have no problem with Velázquez or with Van Dyck ... They can copy them—the more painstakingly the more lucrative it will be ... But instead of allowing the possibility for such a mistake, I'd rather ..."

He searched feverishly through the room, rifled through a few rolls of paper in the armoire, then pulled out a small, curved knife from a drawer. He checked its edge with his finger, and then gestured upwards as if to slash the whole canvas diagonally.

"Mr. McNeill, Mr. McNeill," someone shouted hoarsely from downstairs, "there's a messenger for you. It's a young lady..." Lady V. would have liked very much to find out how the swing of the knife ended, but even more she wanted to know who the messenger was. All that he said, however, was "Thank you Mrs. Culbertson ... Tell her to wait. I'll be down in a minute!"

****

Leaving the Tate, she wandered through a few of the antique shops on the banks of the Thames, happier than ever that in exactly one month her name, at least on paper, would be Mrs. McNeill, although she knew well enough that there was no connection between the young banker with that name who was to be her first husband and the painter whose childhood was spent in the fog—so different from London fog—of Saint Petersburg with its Oriental court etiquette.

It is unnecessary to point out that, however well-educated, Lady V. did not at the time know any more about Whistler than any other well-to-do young lady with an inclination towards the contemplation of paintings in museums. Therefore she could not, then, understand why Sargent, Watts and Fildes, whose paintings she had been taught to admire, should be so marginalized, or that imitating Velázquez or Van Dyck could be less than honorable …

But London offered her so many possibilities to find out more about this, and especially about Whistler himself. And so she did, spending days on end in the overwhelming library at the British Council, then the British Royal Library and finally in the rare manuscripts collection at the Tate Gallery. It so happened that later, in Glasgow, and in Paris, and finally in New York, she was to find scattered but significant traces of the artist's life.

Whoever thinks, though, that Lady V. intended to write a Whistler monograph, or at least a fictionalized biography, is wrong. Whistler had become, simply, a part of her personal life, bland and misunderstood as that was later discovered to be. It's true that she kept a journal, but that turned out in the end to be more a testament to her profound loneliness than the maniacal expression of a passion for Whistler, whose name, nevertheless, appears in it more often that those of all four of her husbands combined. She especially liked to imagine situations in which the painter might have been, based not so much on the details of his biography which Lady V. had come to know in its minutest details, but on the paintings themselves.

It was, therefore, easy for her to assume, a few years later when her official name was no longer McNeill and she was already living in Glasgow, that the messenger was a certain Ms. Dodds who was bringing the painter a letter from Théophile Gautier. Walking back up the creaking stairs, the painter stopped a few times, proof that he had already begun reading the note that let him know that *Symphony in White*, the enigmatic and unfortunate painting that had been so misunderstood by the imbeciles (like that ridiculous association with Wilkie Collins's *Lady in White*!) had once again been rejected by the *Académie* and, continued Gautier, would be shown at the *Salon des Refusés*.[2] The news delighted him: he couldn't ask for better company than Manet and all the other artists who would not bow down to the poor taste of the academics. "The

2 The *Salon des Refusés* was created to appease those painters (Monet, Manet, Pissarro, Whistler, Jongkind and others) who were insulted by the rejection of their works by the official Salon. Artists who had gone against established and acceptable painting techniques were given, for the first time, the right to a public viewing.

imitator is a poor kind of creature … If the man who paints only the tree, or flowers, or other surface he sees before him were an artist, the king of artists would be the photographer," he muttered and laughed, repeating a few times "The photographer, yes, the photographer!" while he shaved off some bumps of paint with the curved knife. We'll never know, thought Lady V., what gesture the knife had been destined for before Mrs. Culbertson announced the arrival of the messenger!

The painter put down the knife, picked up the brush again, and signed in the bottom right corner: *Whistler.* From the easel, the 1872 self-portrait watched him with something ironic and reproachful in its gaze; and opening the notebook with thick leather covers he wrote next to a sketch: *Arrangement in Gray: Portrait of the Painter.*

* * * * * * * * *

It's strange how, even when she was living in London, it was Paris, where she had only been as a child, that seemed so familiar to Lady V. When she realized that, in fact, the self-portrait must have been painted in Paris, and not in London or Glasgow, and that Mrs. Culbertson could just as easily have been named Chambord or Leclerc, just as the messenger, Ms. Dodds, had probably been Mlle. Mazière or Villette, she felt relieved of the need to be as exact as possible—her attempts in any case were prone to possess her before she had a chance to impose anything upon them! This isn't what mattered at all.

In this way she returned easily to the scene where it seemed to her that the self-portrait would be slashed diagonally with that curved and probably very sharp knife.

Many years had passed since then. Lady V. had settled in New York sometime in the early 60s, but no one could have noticed the passing of time on her face, even if she had ever been immortalized in a portrait, because she was, as we have already mentioned, almost unchanged in forty years. She herself had become used to this. She no longer even received any compliments at the rare reunions of the Guggenheim, Rockefeller or Roth foundations that she sometimes attended mostly out of curiosity, and where no one would have thought to say: "Oh Lady V. you look so ... *unchanged*!", when such compliments generally referred exactly to some detail that was especially changed. But, in her case, there didn't seem to be anything worth complimenting, neither generally nor in detail.

This could perhaps also be part of Whistler's influence, or of the obstinacy of the American South that spoke through the whole being of this daughter of Yankee *arrivistes* who had managed nonetheless to illustrate the survival of an archetype, protected equally from the erosion of time and from the joy and petty satisfactions of a more common life.

You could ask yourself, and rightfully so, if Lady V. would not have wanted to eventually also live in Washington, where there are not only the Whistlers at the *National Gallery*, but also the far from negligible paintings at the *Freer Collection* and especially the famous *Peacock Room*, brought from London and restored. Lady V. had, in fact, the opportunity to see *The*

Peacock Room in its different incarnations, and sometimes even allowed herself the luxury of going back in time to try to figure out what exactly had caused the irreconcilable argument between the painter and Mr. Leyland, the owner of a valuable and quite varied collection of Asian art that betrayed, more than anything else, the tendency of businessmen towards a passion for possessing *exotic goods* as she called them in the journal. Only a businessman's (even an English one's!) lack of subtlety could have so blindly satisfied the pride of the ship-owner from Liverpool immortalized by Whistler in *Arrangement in Black: Portrait of F.R. Leyland*, so as to not notice the obvious. Lady V. had always considered the painting, aside from its nod to portraiture, a bit of mockery: the small head, the inexpressive eyes under a narrow forehead, the magisterial position of the body, like some low Spanish noble in a portrait by Velázquez ...

****

As soon as Frederick Leyland left, Whistler returned to the enormous sitting room, designed so carefully by Thomas Jeckyll. It was clear that the architect had taken his job very seriously, even going beyond the call of duty to make all those Chinese vases conform to an environment that was unsuitable, if not outright hostile, to them ... And above everything else, in place of pride above the fireplace *La Princesse du Pays de la Porcelaine*, Whistler's painting from 1864, which seemed to have come from another lifetime! He remembered exactly how he had made the frame—in those days he painted all his frames—and thought, with a touch of panic, how inappropriately his paintings would be displayed that day, or the next, or after a century, or ten, in different corners of the world. A little while later he felt much better drinking, slowly and deliberately, a glass of port from Leyland's select collection.

He walked distractedly through the room, trying to figure out the one thing that was … off. Jeckyll himself had sensed it, being a man of good taste and talent—Leyland didn't deserve him, thought Whistler. Actually, it was only at the architect's insistence that Leyland had decided to consult the painter on the décor, as he himself thought Jeckyll's version to be magnificent. At any rate, Thomas Jeckyll, if for no other reason than out of reverence for the painting above the fireplace, insisted that Whistler give his opinion on the room. "Ha ha," Whistler laughed to himself, warmed by the alcohol and about to have one of those revelations, "this is perhaps what separates a man of taste from a clod: even if he doesn't know *exactly* what is wrong, he will always know that some detail sounds a discordant note, then leave the artist himself to determine what that might be and what is to be done … What is to be done …."

Not for the first time Whistler realized he felt extremely comfortable in the house at 49 Prince's Gate. And this not just because of his arrogance—which, there is no doubt, was quite large—at being around his own painting. Actually, he considered *La Princesse du Pays de la Porcelaine*, with all the overwhelming exoticism of its décor and the princess's clothing, an experiment he had moved past long ago. Lady V. who, as we have already mentioned, often visited Leyland's sitting room, had entered that particular painting a few times, and the only thing that sent a shiver down her spine was not the sumptuous clothing (that was in any case a combination of a few different styles from different eras) but the vague expression on her face, as if Whistler had deliberately blurred it around the forehead, the eyes, and at the bridge of the nose which, otherwise, was contoured quite firmly, as were the chin, cheekbones, neck, and hairline. Maybe just this unsettling detail juxtaposed with the sunny splendor of the entire composition down to the gold frame redeemed that whole painting.

"Gold! Gold! Gold!" Whistler found himself shouting while stumbling through the room after his second glass of port, and Lady V. smiled, not without a trace of worry, because she knew what would come next. In three days, Jeckyll's entire vision of the sitting room would be discarded and expensive leather, gold ornaments, peacock feathers and rare wood with mother-of-pearl inlay would take the place of the more routine deliveries made to the imposing house at 49 Prince's Gate. Nobody was allowed in the room. Whistler worked alone from morning till night, gold-leafing the walls and ceiling, adding peacock feathers and laurel leaves, ceaselessly moving the pottery stands designed by Jeckyll and rearranging the Chinese vases on them, looking for the perfect combination, the one, among all others, that felt *necessary*. And all this after he had promised Leyland that he would only adjust a few details, a day or two of work, something that the rich man had finally agreed to before leaving for Liverpool—just a few fragments here and there!—though he considered the room already perfect.

All the feverish work, Lady V. noticed, stopped every evening around ten o'clock when the gas light went off in the living room only to re-appear in the East wing of the house, Mrs. Leyland's apartment. Mrs. Leyland, that enigmatic and fragile silhouette that floated more than walked, almost always engrossed in a book or listening to music; she herself probably one of those *exotic goods* that Leyland was so proud of owning... These were the moments when, following in the footsteps of the artist who had just left what was to become the celebrated *Peacock Room*, Lady V. entered the sitting room, noting with as much delight as fear all the changes from one day to the next, walking into the painting *La Princesse du Pays de la Porcelaine*, or simply falling asleep on the leather sofa in front of the fireplace.

It so happened that Lady V. herself, without being able to explain exactly why, also felt extremely comfortable in the rich London residence at 49 Prince's Gate.

****

As much as Whistler tried to keep Leyland away from London and from the sitting room that was becoming less and less *his*, one day this one returned out of the blue. Among other things, Lady V. quotes a letter in which Whistler begs him not to come back from Liverpool until "the ensemble shines in all its perfection," something "really alive with beauty—brilliant and gorgeous while at the same time delicate and refined to the last degree." Words that, one can imagine, did more to worry than to reassure the businessman!

We can assume that, from that day forward, the precious deliveries to 49 Prince's Gate came to an abrupt end, as did the light after ten or eleven o'clock in Mrs. Leyland's apartment, but it would be fairly difficult to know the link between these two details, if any. The only clear thing was Leyland's violent reaction when he discovered that all this trifling *adjustment of details* was going to cost him 2,000 guineas. In the meantime, Whistler, radiant and delighted with the room's balance, had shown it to a large number of visitors, critics and journalists, so that it would have been difficult at that point for its owner to object (leaving aside his dubious competence for doing so...).

In the end, Leyland offered to pay him half the commission he had asked for and did not hesitate to insult him by paying the amount in pounds, the market currency, instead of in guineas, the currency in which artists used to be paid. Whistler did not allow such an affront to go unnoticed, avenging himself by recreating, on the wall opposite *La Princesse du Pays de la Porcelaine*, a fight between two peacocks wearing elements which make them more than recognizable. The aggressive peacock wears silver feathers around his neck, an allusion to the shirts with this kind of decoration that Frederick Leyland was fond of; the other one has white feathers on its head, an obvious nod to the unmistakable streak of silver on Whistler's own forehead. There is a bunch of shillings scattered on the ground at the Leyland peacock's feet ... As if all this had not been enough, and knowing his client's obtuseness, Whistler named the fresco *Art and Money; or, The Story of the Room*. After laying diagonally across the room a blue carpet of the appropriate, slightly Vermeerian shade, in March 1877 Whistler considered his work done, named the whole thing *Harmony in Blue and Gold*, and never saw it again to his dying day.

Lady V., however, returned often to the sitting room at 49 Prince's Gate in the time before it was called *The Peacock Room* and before all the conflict with Leyland. When, even before the war, Lady V. saw it in Washington, where Charles Lang Freer had had it transported in 1904, the room had seemed to exude insufferable animosities and an artificial air. So she decided to travel backwards to relive the delightful feelings of that whole period, especially when, after Whistler left and the lights went on in the ethereal apartment of Mrs. Leyland, she could look over all that fascinating décor, reborn with every new day.

In the end, she could never figure out the true roots of the irreconcilable conflict between Whistler and Leyland—if it had perhaps been something more than the story with the money.

* * * * * * * * * * * *

"Art, and therefore life itself, do not have much to do with what is required from without. I prefer to name my canvases compositions of color rather than portraits or landscapes, even at the risk that the composition will show tragic misunderstanding or incompatibility. At least this disaster, as it is, will portray a true encounter, unmediated by compromises or fashion!"

This quote from Lady V.'s journal (copied from or cobbled together using phrases from several of the painter's articles?) takes one of Whistler's cardinal ideas to an extreme that even he, perhaps, would not want. It is just as true, however, that Whistler tended towards such extremes. It is phrases like these that must have so stunned Oscar Wilde—who, no matter what else may be said about him, was not an easy man to stun!—that he exclaimed, in black and white for all to see, in *The Decay of Lying*: "But you don't mean to say that you seriously believe that Life imitates Art, that Life in fact is the mirror, and Art the reality?"

Strange that Wilde would be shocked, noted Lady V., when he had surprised his contemporaries in so many ways with his eccentricities and behavior outside of any norm, and especially as the writer of *The Picture of Dorian Gray*... In regards to Whistler, however, such things applied not only as grand statements, but also as actual facts: hadn't he changed his own biography so many times, affirming that he had been born either in Saint Petersburg, where, true enough, he had spent a few years in his childhood, or in Baltimore, but never in the provincial and dusty town of Lowell, Massachusetts, where the event had actually taken place in 1834?... So his declaration in *The Gentle Art of Making Enemies*—that he should have been born exactly where and when he wished, and it just so happens that this place would not, under any circumstances, have been Lowell!—comes as no great surprise. Lady V. found this statement especially touching, bringing her sometimes to tears as it pointed, at least in her way of judging things, to his painful need to reunify his scattered self.

* * * * * * * * * * * * *

Clearly someone like Lady V., who was so intensely preoccupied by these discoveries of the past, had little time to worry
about such insignificant and ultimately disappointing details as
her first husband's ruined fortune, subsequent bankruptcy, suicide, a new marriage and a move to Glasgow followed by a
divorce and, after only two years, settling in Paris…

Lady V. hadn't been to Paris since she was a child, when her
parents had for some or all purposes ignored her, preoccupied
as they were with so much worldliness and expensive purchas-
es to be made in the shops on *Rive Droite*. She had decided to
take this trip—after the extremely civilized divorce she
obtained without any opposition from Phil Kaplan and that left
her with a more than generous sum—with the secret intention
of discovering the *city of lights* in the same way that Whistler
had discovered it a century earlier. She had not intended to stay
longer than two weeks, and only the strange circumstances
under which she met Michel Villefort and the well-known
promise that she subsequently made would tie her to Paris for
the next ten years of her life.

Climbing up *rue Lepic* to the immense *Sacré Cœur* cathe-
dral that dominates the landscape like a giant meringue and
that wouldn't even have been there a hundred years before, she
tried to imagine today's bland *Montmartre* in a completely different light. For hours she searched fruitlessly for Gleyre's former studio. He was Whistler's first master when, freshly arrived

in Paris, the latter was more inclined to support the gentle tyranny of this Swiss painter who, despite being trained in the academic tradition, encouraged his students' creative iconoclasms, than to waste his time at the *Ecole des Beaux-Arts* where the servants of French Academism were busy polishing the corpse of modern painting which they themselves had killed. She soon found out that Gleyre's studio had been torn down a long time ago. Nonetheless, she could imagine it somewhere out there, even the shuffling of painters setting up their easels and mixing pigments under the direction of the Swiss man. She could see them all: Bazille, Renoir, Monet and, somewhere in the shadows, the young American frowning and trying out a dozen brushes—Gleyre's obsession that each brush represents a dominant color on the palette!—and probably still hesitating between either embracing the bohemian with all its trappings or showing off the much sought-after and fascinating sobriety of a dandy ... The multiple brush motif was to follow Whistler throughout his professional life, and, forty years later, as an instructor at the Carmen Academy he would encourage his students to give their brushes women's names such as "Suzanna" or "Maria" in order to distinguish them more easily. Would he have advised any of them, wondered Lady V. not without a trace of meanness, to use the name Maud? Even in Paris she could not shake the animosity, rare for her, that she felt towards this name—not even towards the woman herself, but towards the paintings.

Walking back down towards *La Madeleine*, Lady V. tried to imagine the city, having just escaped from the trauma of the revolution and the fall of the second Republic in 1851, on the threshold of a new hope of reconstruction fueled by the promises of Napoleon III and his Second Empire. The mayor of Paris was none other than Baron Haussmann who would become, despite all opposition, the true architect of the Paris of today with its boulevards whose width seemed, at the time, an exaggeration, its buildings over ten stories tall, and its sumptuous bridges. De Tocqueville's nostalgia for the hodge-podge of the old market town was being supplanted by those like Baudelaire who enthusiastically asked that artists glorify the heroism of modern life. Urbanity would, in fact, shortly make an appearance in Baudelaire's poetry, and the fragment in "La Revue" from 1845 in which he addresses painters is very relevant: "The painter, the true painter for whom we are looking, will be he who can snatch its epic quality from the life of today and can make us see and understand, with brush or with pencil, how great and poetic we are in our cravats and patent-leather boots." And were not these artists already working? Manet, Degas, Pissarro, Monet, Caillebotte all engaged in the irreconcilable conflict between the numbing and uncompromising academism promoted by the *Ecole des Beaux-Arts* and the various Salons that dedicated themselves to the radical ideas expressed by Courbet and later Manet and the Impressionists. And how well Whistler himself had followed Baudelaire's advice if we were only to look at the portrait of Duret! Lady V. often imagined them all, especially as they appeared in Fantin-Latour's painting, a canvas which she had entered many times more in the interest of understanding her own identity than in an attempt to scrutinize each and every one of them as they were thoroughly depicted there.[3]

* * * * * * * * * * * * * *

Back to the journal: Lady V. notes that in 1855, at the time Whistler arrived in this ideologically divided city, the conflict between old and new was about to be resolved by the juxtaposition of both at the opening of the Universal Exposition. She tried uselessly to imagine the surprising mix of international industry, commerce, and art. However, she had no trouble seeing the heterogeneous bazaar at the Porte de Clignancourt, so much so that, at one point, she thought it strange that she did not shock people with her modern clothing. She realized then that she was probably invisible—even though the whole thing was extremely vivid, without a hint of fantasy!—and could go about exploring the two huge pavilions. The first one housed the academics and showed, among others, painting by Delacroix and Ingres; the other one, much smaller but still a veritable citadel, had the inscription *Realism. G. Courbet*. She entered the latter to admire one more time the celebrated *Artist's Studio* even though she knew that the canvas now resides at the Louvre. She examined minutely the details of this painting she knew would so fascinate and move Whistler to the point that he would, for a while, relocate from Gleyer's studio to that of Bonvin where he could work with Courbet to his

[3] Lady V. alludes here to *Homage à Delacroix*, 1864, that shows Fantin-Latour himself, with Baudelaire, Manet, Bazille, Whistler, and others grouped round a portrait of Delacroix.

heart's content. His enthusiasm for pure realism, however, was not to last and perhaps Courbet's doctrinarian tendencies were also not to his liking. This convinced him to found, along with Fantin-Latour and Alphonse Legros, the *Society of the Three* started under their boundless reverence for Courbet but later leading to *une expérience de passage* that would take each of them on his own distinct path.

Sometimes Lady V. thought that, for Whistler, Paris would have been nothing more than an intriguing pretext had it not been for his friendships with Montesquiou, Duret, and Fantin-Latour. In the end, the influence of Courbet's realism produced nothing but the remarkable self-portrait where the young artist wears a large black hat (and that, really, is influenced as much by Courbet as by Rembrandt) and the unforgettable *La Mère Gérard,* a replica of Manet's absinthe drinker. Lady V. even attempted in a few lines of her journal to imagine the small lending library where *La Mère Gérard* would have felt, before its demolition, like a true owner—something she might very well have been!—then tried to see her today. And, indeed, found somehow her descendents among the old women who sold flowers in the Jardin d'Luxembourg with the devastatingly resigned expression seen on Whistler's canvas and that perpetual and unanswerable *Why?* on their face...

She definitely had more trouble imagining other scenes from Whistler's Parisian life. It would be hard to say, based solely on the journal, that Lady V. was jealous of any of the painter's many well-known "flames", but she was obsessed with one and only one name: Maud Franklin. Often Lady V.

didn't even know how to picture her: the frivolous girl in *Arrangement in White and Black: The Young American*, or the emancipated young lady imagining herself a *grand dame* in *The Fur Jacket*. These two paintings she had never entered.

****

Whistler walked slowly down *rue du Sabot*. The meeting with Duret had been the only productive thing he had done all day. His eventual break with Courbet seemed more and more inevitable: he couldn't live on respect and consideration alone. He would go back to London and try, maybe, to explain it to Fantin-Latour in a longish letter ... or maybe once he got to London and away from Paris he would actually rediscover Courbet. Everything in Paris was too much a part of the predictable décor: the people, the paintings, the ideas. Their *Society* had obviously lost its meaning. It was clear that all the subtle distinctions to which even he sometimes had fallen victim, and in which he would find himself trapped as in a thicket, were actually empty of any content. In the end, he told himself, the history of the beautiful is already complete—hewn in the marbles of the Parthenon—and broidered, with the birds, upon the fan of Hokusai—at the foot of Fusiyama.

Turning toward *Montparnasse*, he could not help but notice that time itself had acquired a material, almost palpable quality, and that he could distinguish, just then, the reluctant passing of the seconds that would have wanted to be returned to the certainty of their womb, in the morning, rather than continue toward an evening that promised to lead nowhere. Breathing became difficult, as if he had something stuck in his throat; he felt a weight on his chest and the curious illusion that he was outside his own body, watching himself walk up *rue Vaugirard* and experiencing that strange feeling.

All this lasted only a moment and, not much later, Lady V. could see him walking into the lobby of *Hotel Lutèce*. "You have a letter," said the receptionist at the desk stopping him, "and Mrs. Whistler stopped by looking for you. She said she'll be waiting for you at 9 o'clock at *La Rotonde*." "Very well! I hope that is all," mumbled the painter, still confused by that sensation of the grittiness of time. "Please make sure I'm not disturbed." He ran up the stairs as he always did, but now he seemed shaken and could not wait to throw himself on his bed, which is exactly what he did a few moments later.

Lady V. was annoyed: imagine that! *Mrs. Whistler!* That Maud Franklin had no shame! Just appeared and disappeared whenever she felt like it and, on top of everything else, was now calling herself *Mrs. Whistler*. Maud had begun modeling for him when she was only sixteen years old and since then had been hanging around him whenever she had the chance. All the excursions—to Venice, the Azure Coast—the bohemian life she shared with Whistler in London, even the two children she eventually had or the minor fame she achieved as a painter working under a borrowed name; none of these things bothered Lady V. as much as the gall of calling herself *Mrs. Whistler*... and of course the two paintings *The White Fur*, and *Arrangement in White and Black: The Young American* which was later acquired by Freer and transported to Washington (this only served to increase Lady V.'s dislike of that city).

Maud had stopped referring to herself in this manner only in 1888 when Whistler married Beatrix Godwin, the only official *Mrs. Whistler*. At least for the few years they had together, for she was to die of cancer in 1896. Lady V. felt no animosity towards *this* Mrs. Whistler. Quite the opposite, she felt for her a sort of compassion mixed with who knows what, perhaps respect.

Lady V. imagined Whistler sleeping in his room at the *Lutèce*, trying to leave behind the feelings that had so disturbed him on *rue Vaugirard*. And at *La Rotonde* Maud would probably be nervously smoking one cigarette after another while waiting. "She can wait as long as she wants," thought Lady V. knowing that he would not wake until the next morning when he would hastily pack a few items, leaving the bulk of his things to be shipped to London later. At least for now she knew he was safe!

But all this was just an illusion. In fact, Maud was not at *La Rotonde* at all. She was only fifteen years old and would not even meet Whistler for another year! These small falsehoods had been creeping into Lady V.'s reveries, rarely, it's true, but significantly, and they almost always had to do with Maud Franklin or, more specifically, with the Maud in *The Young American*.

One can assume that another ten years of Lady V.'s life passed in this way, and there is nothing in the journal to contradict this. She leaves Paris, as we have already mentioned, immediately after the death of that gentle Michel Villefort...

For someone who had traveled so much, it is strange that after she established herself in New York she would never again leave America. The journal mentions only a few weeks spent in Massachusetts, but not, as one might expect, in Lowell where Whistler had been born though he refused to acknowledge the fact. To Lady V. it would have seemed a grave injustice to his memory to visit that town, moreover a sign of indifference, which, as we all know, is the unique true opposite of love...

Based on the scant information in the journal, it's safe to assume that she visited the Boston Museum of Fine Arts, the Isabelle Steward Gardner Museum, the elegant Fogg Art Museum in Cambridge, and the cute little galleries in Worcester and Andover. Though there are more Whistler paintings in these few museums than are spread about in all of Philadelphia, Cincinnati, Detroit, Pittsburgh, Farmington, Chicago, even Birmingham, Alabama put together, Lady V. says she did not particularly enjoy seeing those canvases she had only ever seen as reproductions. Some, like *Nocturne in Blue and Silver: Venice Lagoon* and *The Blue Wave: Biarritz*, she liked very much and had even entered on occasion, but only in art books. It is clear here that her emotions were very much in tune with Whistler and what he would have wanted, namely to forget completely that he had been born and lived for a time in Massachusetts. As for Washington, there were not only the strange emotions she experienced when viewing *The Peacock Room*, which she much preferred in its original state at 49 Prince's Gate, but also *Arrangement in White and Black: The Young American*, in other words, the insufferable Maud Franklin...

Her time in New York, however, was not an exile. The Rehnquist family, into which she had entered with the same ease with which she entered Whistler's paintings, was part of the American "aristocracy." Those who doubt this classification can easily search through the pages of the journal or through my own research to realize that we are talking here about upper class intellectuals who paid little attention to the tedium of everyday life, nonchalantly spending their inherited fortune on anything that would make their lives more comfortable, and contributing generously to all sorts of lost or soon-to-be-lost causes. The apartment on Madison and 79th Street often saw the likes of Andy Warhol, Lenny Bernstein, John Updike, William Saroyan, Philip Roth, and sometimes no less than Jacqueline Kennedy even before the death of Peter Lars Rehnquist, Lady V.'s fourth and last husband. That being said, it would not be right of us to lay the blame of snobbery on Lady V. for these get-togethers (which she saw as her way of lastly making peace with the North).

Pages after pages in the journal are devoted to her discovery of not only Manhattan (where the Metropolitan Museum of Art and the Frick Collection would become daily haunts), but of the great variety of the city, from the foul-smelling streets of Chinatown to the quaint shops in Little Italy and Soho, and from the Jewish neighborhoods in Brooklyn where she often went to eat blintzes or pickles to the modest Greek and Cypriot cafes in Astoria where the smell of gyros mixed perfectly with the slightly sour taste of the white wine and the knocking dice of the backgammon players. Lady V. was discovering the profound humanity of these simple, plebeian pleasures for which she had a natural and, without knowing exactly why, nostalgic admiration. Sometimes she walked home from the Cypriot tavern at the end of Ditmars Boulevard, passing the Greek dry cleaner by the name of *Katharsis*, and then walking through the impossible racket on the Queensborough Bridge which never failed to put her into a panic that ended only when she came out in Manhattan at 59th Street.

****

She had been going to the Frick Collection, that elegant palace on the corner of 5th Avenue and 70th Street, every day for twenty years, with the exception of several short periods when the museum was closed for renovations and Mondays when the museum is always closed. She appreciated its size (much less overwhelming that the Metropolitan, Guggenheim, or the Museum of Modern Art), as well as the style of this "personal" collection where different periods and styles blended together—from the sun-drenched Turners to the crepuscular Gainsborough, from Rembrandt's ravishing, late self-portrait to the grandeur of El Greco, from the metaphysics in the portraits of Holbein or Memling to the enigmas in Vermeer's paintings, the rare enamels from Limoges, or the "earthiness" of the air in Corot's canvases…

Was not this collection a boundless celebration of beauty in all its variations, just as Whistler himself would have liked? Not to even mention the five Whistler paintings that were housed here and constituted, in her words, the final element in the harmony of this small *oecumene*, as Lady V. calls the place in a phrase of the journal.

That sunny and warm Friday morning in October didn't seem at all special, except maybe for the multilingual buzz that surrounded her in all of the galleries: the late autumn had presumably brought out more tourists than in other years and Lady V. almost envied those who were discovering the wonders at the Frick for the first time. She enjoyed watching their reactions closely and then judging the wealth or poverty of their souls based just on those reactions…

As she walked through this Tower of Babel, the conversation between two men caught her attention. They were walking slowly in front of the paintings, then stopping suddenly and turning this way and that, presumably to get a better angle. At first Lady V. found all this conspicuous movement repellent, especially since the shorter of the two was in the habit of removing and replacing his glasses over and over, and made huge, dramatic gestures with his hands as he spoke. The other one concentrated on the paintings, occasionally taking notes. Coming closer to them, Lady V. found them more agreeable when she discovered the sincere delight on their faces and the fervor with which they took in every detail. It was obvious that the shorter man was familiar with the museum (perhaps that is why he talked so much), while the other allowed himself to be led through the rooms looking dreamily but intensely at the art, answering now and then, and showing unreserved admiration for what he saw.

Lady V. understood almost everything they said, but after deciding that they were not speaking English, she could not determine exactly what language they were speaking. Sometimes it took her a while to realize that people were not speaking English, precisely because she *understood* what they were saying. She had shown a great talent for languages even as a child. Old Jemima taught her two Creole dialects when she was about nine years old. When she had been living in Glasgow she studied German, Icelandic and some Celtic dialects, and in Paris she took classes in the Romance languages at the *Sorbonne* without ever intending to get a diploma. She had also learned a bit of Polish and Russian and, in New York, took lessons in Modern Greek. She decided that the visitors, whom she was now practically following, were speaking some sort of Retro-Roman (she had taken a course in Romance dialects at Aix-en-Provence), although it could have just as easily been a form of Latin, a bit modernized and spoken with a Slavic accent.

"Retro-Roman or not," she said to herself, "God must know what it is because I understand it!" The journal shows evidence of one of her earlier attempts to justify the existence of God through a linguistic argument as she called it (it is unclear if she was aware of Borges' famous *ornithologist argument*). "It happens to me sometimes," wrote Lady V., "that I find myself thinking for hours in a language that I do not know, though I recognize it as fully intelligible. If the language is strictly determined and I understand it, then it must be one of the languages that I know and God may or may not exist. Sometimes I think maybe that it's Polish, but it isn't Polish, or French, Portuguese, or Spanish; it isn't Russian, or Italian, or English, or German; it isn't any one of the Romance or Celtic dialects I have studied and it's definitely not Icelandic. It seems like it's a little bit of each and at the same time none of them. But such a language could not exist; therefore God must exist!"

****

They were definitely well-educated men—most likely writers based on the *epic*, literary comments they made about every painting. Lady V. could not suppress her typically Whistlerian horror at the way in which they, especially the shorter one, imposed entire stories onto canvases that simply *existed* as harmony of colors and nothing else! She left them for a little while turning into the courtyard where the bubbling of the fountains always soothed her. She was looking at Whistler's small painting *Symphony in Gray and Green: The Ocean*. With its subtle shades of green, blue and gray, it was like therapy for a fevered mind looking to get away from the narrative...

Without any warning she found herself entering the painting, trading in the calm babbling of the fountains in the elegant little courtyard for the rhythmic crashing of the massive waves in the painting. Taking a few steps, she noticed two figures approaching and then retreating at the far end of the beach, as if playing a game. She ran toward them as quickly as she could with her heavy shoes on the damp sand. She was instantly able to distinguish the white plume on the barefoot Whistler's forehead blowing in the breeze. And with him, carrying her sandals in her hand, with her skirt indecently tied into a knot underneath her large breasts to keep it out of the water and wearing a lavender shirt that seemed to have been thrown on hastily, was none other than Maud Franklin! This was the first time that Lady V. saw her like this: not as the coquette young girl from *Arrangement in White and Black* or the pretentious lady from *The Fur Jacket*, but simply as a woman, as Whitsler's mistress, a main character in that never-ending adventure…

She left the painting, more annoyed than ever with herself, feeling as if she had committed an act of *hubris*, not against Whistler, but against her own dignity. Was there anything more ridiculous than being jealous of a transient woman who was nothing more than big breasts and long legs? Who promised only a certain type of passion that Mrs. V. had refused or that had been refused her so many times by then? And all this in front of one of Whistler's canvases! The crime of *lèse-peinture*, as she called it in her journal, made her feel guiltier than anything else and she decided to leave *The Ocean* and the courtyard immediately.

Returning to the last room on the left side of the courtyard she was pleased to run into the two gentlemen whom she had lost for a while. Passing by the portrait of *Lisa Corder* they stopped in front of *Black and Gold: Le Comte Robert Montesquiou*. And how much they had to say about something that should have been seen as nothing more than an arrangement of colors! The taller one hastened to mention the strangeness of the composition, so in tune with the personality of its subject, that *D'Artagnan du rare et de l'exquis* who would, or so the man claimed, inspire no less than three famous literary characters: Proust's *Baron Charlus*, Huysmans's *Des Esseintes*, and Lorrains' *Monsieur de Phocas*. "Obscure incarnations, no doubt," added the shorter of the two. Lady V. notes in her journal that, leaving aside, of course, their admiration for Whistler's mastery—such as it was, filtered through their narrative arguments—their entire conversation was frivolous and ostentatiously *intellectual*.

She had often entered this painting which had been so controversial as far back as 1892. In Glasgow, she had read the original letter from Montesquiou to Whistler in which the count had promised to bring him a small surprise from London. A surprise that turned out to be the interminable poem *Moth* in which (she realized just now) Montesquiou evoked all the paintings that would eventually end up at the Frick. She had memorized two stanzas and she recited them to herself right there, no longer following the conversation of the two gentlemen:

Car sa touche se puise au sein vrai de la vie;
Pas un trait ne s'empreint hormis que bien vital,
Et nostre lassitude à poser est suivie
D'un lever de nous mêmes au cadre de métal!

Ces yeux que nul n'a fait voir comme en tes peintures,
Les yeux du deuil des nuits, ces yeux du seuil des jours;
Ces yeux auxquels to dis, dans la pose qui dure:
Regardez-moi ce peu, pour regarder toujours![4]

The last line alludes to a real event that happened while Montesquiou was posing for Whistler. We do not want to bore the reader with a fragment of a journal within a journal, but I must mention that Lady V. transcribed the following section from Montesquiou's notes and as, presumably, it must have happened in real life: "So, after almost inciting, in his painting, a meeting of Poe's Wilson with his *döppelganger*, of Shelley's Zoroaster with himself, or of Musset with that youth who wore all black and who resembled him like a brother—after all this synthesis to be found in the painting, he turned suddenly to me

[4] Because his touch is drawn from life's true breast;
Not a tree is imprinted except the very rare
And to post what follows our laziness
Is a lifting of ourselves to the metal square!
....
By night, the eyes of eyries, by day those eyes of yes;
Those eyes were never made to see, as in your oeuvre;
Those eyes to whom you say, in the enduring pose
Look at me a moment, so as to look forever!
(Translation by Jeffrey Jullich, *The Transcendental Friend*, No.9, September 1999)

and, throwing me a triumphant look, he uttered possibly the most beautiful phrase ever uttered by a painter: *Look at me one more time, and you'll be looking at me forever!*" Lady V. then goes on to comment on her reservations about the non-Whistlerian way in which the real Montesquiou (about whom, in her opinion, there was nothing demonic except maybe that artificial *persona* projected and maintained by himself with so much effort) treats the entire creation of the painting which should not even be thought of as anything but *Black and Gold*... Some apocryphal notes she had borrowed from one of the count's nephews in Bourges indicate that, after Whistler uttered his famous phrase, Montesquiou lowered his gaze, turned suddenly and fled down the stairs of the artist's studio. "I felt that if I listened to him and looked at him for even one second more, I would be sucked forever into the painting!"

****

In the meantime, the two men had reached the other end of the room where *Harmony in Pink and Gray: Lady Meux* and *Symphony in Flesh Color and Pink: Mrs. Leyland* hang. They were moving so quickly and conspicuously from one painting to another, it would have been difficult not to watch them. The short man especially seemed to have an entire presentation prepared, but his friend did not appear to be too convinced either by the words or by the ample gestures which accompanied them. Lady V. walked toward them, irresistibly attracted, as she was to confess, even though she had already decided that nothing they had said was of any value.

"Trust me. I know what I'm saying. I've looked at these paintings a thousand times: he certainly made love to Lady Meux, though he was later profoundly disappointed. Mrs. Leyland he loved platonically and with much respect, which must have made him suffer a lot!"

"Such speculations," the tall one replied, "should be based on something, and the fact that you've seen the paintings a thousand times does not validate your theory. I find both these portraits absolutely fascinating, each in its own way, and I don't see why you need to create an artificial paradox or fantasize about things that are hard to prove…"

Lady V. could not help but agree completely with this assessment.

"But it is a matter of evidence," the other one started in. "Look at *Lady Meux*: it's obvious that her body is something to be envied with its long legs, large breasts, narrow waist; look at those pouty, greedy lips, the sensual nose. But notice also the stare in her eyes: this is a woman who knows what and how much she wants from the man she's with. And what remains *after*? After it is just the ridiculous disaster when, for a terrible period of time, there is nothing left to say or do, nothing but mortified flesh! Look again at her fixed gaze, at the touch of awkwardness: nothing there indicates a union! Poor Whistler, he must have been very depressed *after*. Though, this didn't stop him from later wanting her again and even passionately possessing her only to fall prey to the same hopelessness, afterwards. While here," he said, turning towards *Mrs. Leyland*'s portrait, "we see something completely different. Look how every detail seems to breathe with life. Though, I ask you, how many times have you seen a woman painted from the back? Look how her hands, joined together behind her back, form a perfect chalice. Her whole dress looks like it was woven out of air, and look at the ethereal flowers on it and how they evoke so well the Japanese cherry branch in the left hand corner of the painting. How many women painted from the back could say that they are superb, perfect because of the beauty that they hide? Turn your attention now to the semi-profile of the face, with its firm features, not marked by any sign of sensuality. But still, her formless body posed in this way, covered by an immaterial dress that makes it almost impossible to figure out what is on the other side, or imagine the full figure of this woman of which we see only a fragment—doesn't all this create a sensual tension that is above that of common trappings like large breasts, fleshy lips, or a well-defined waist? Yes, I'm telling you, a thousand times yes, and Whistler never resisted the temptation, in his paintings or in life, to leave that tension there, even to nurture it (at the same time nurturing his own suffering) and glorify that which is most profound in femininity: sensitivity, understanding, beauty beyond form, and eternally unspoken love!"

Despite how pathetic these sentences were, Lady V. was deeply disturbed. She felt as if she were in danger, as if someone or something that had been protecting her for a long time was just about to disappear forever. She did not know what could be beyond this experience, but a voice told her that it could not be anything good. She hadn't felt so threatened since childhood, but those fears were rational and easy to decipher, while now she felt like she was about to find out something she did not want to and, more importantly, was never meant to know.

"Let's turn back to *Lady Meux*. What would be left of her if she had been painted from the back? Try to imagine that Whistler had painted her in exactly the same position as *Mrs. Leyland*. I'll tell you what you'd be left with: common, large hips, a much less defined waist and, instead of the large breasts, a somewhat vulgar profile above the rounded shoulders, the nostrils almost quivering with sensuality, an inexpressive fragment of her forehead, and perhaps that same empty look: that is certainly no compliment! The gorgeous *Lady Meux*! And please, don't tell me that one could just as easily ruin any painting in this way!"

"But," continued the other one with some hesitation, "what if we were to apply the same treatment to the other portrait, *Mrs. Leyland's*? Why couldn't we try to imagine her painted by Whistler in the same position as *Lady Meux*?"

Lady V. would have liked to stop them, to scream, or even to drive them away from their using any of the languages she knew, or, even better, the one that they were speaking and that she understood so well. But something stronger stood in her way forcing her to keep following their conversation.

"Because, my dear friend," responded the short one triumphantly as they both walked back towards the portrait of *Mrs. Leyland*. "Here it couldn't change anything. You can paint her any way you want. All you have to do is turn her head so that she is looking at you straight on and nothing else: notice that the back could just as easily be the chest given the vague way in which it is outlined. But what you could see on that face, that's something else entirely! If I'm right, and Whistler imagined her as the very nature of femininity, you couldn't look at her face for too long anyway. You would simply fall helplessly and forever in love with her and you would advance towards the painting like a sleepwalker until, touching the canvas, you would set off the alarm and the security guards, after having handcuffed you, would be more likely to hand you over to a psychiatric hospital than to the police!"

****

The last pages of Lady V.'s journal end with Mallarmé's sonnet *Sainte*, whose last verse talks of the enigmatic *musicienne du silence*. After all the other elements of the music that once had resounded in the room dissipate, the harp is suddenly brought to life by the flight of an angel on whose invisible wings the delicate chords intone silence … Surely the atmosphere associated with her distress on that October morning in the Frick must have motivated her to include it here.

After the two gentlemen's departure she was left in a kind of stupor and only the preparations for the closing of the museum at five o'clock brought her back to her senses. She didn't want to leave even though she knew or rather she kept trying to convince herself, that all that they said—and how many

conversations had she listened to over the years in museums!—had nothing to do with her. She realized that for a few
hours now she hadn't been looking at either of the two paintings, but where she had been all this time she could not say.
She was fed up and ready to leave when the security guard
began walking towards her. She hated these scenes which she
had seen in so many museums: tourists dead set on a sort of
cultural treasure hunt obtaining, after tedious explanations and
laments, another ten minutes to see this or that so that they can
tick it off the list and go, as empty as they had come, to a
restaurant or the Empire State Building or *The Blue Note* in the
Village or simply back to their hotel...

The guard, who knew her well, told her that the museum
would remain open until nine that day, but that she must leave
the room for a half hour as a Japanese millionaire and owner
of, among other things, an art magazine, wanted to devote an
entire issue to the Frick and the photographer was about to
shoot the paintings in that room. Turning her head, she noticed
that indeed an entire army of specialists were setting up
tripods. Mechanically, she headed towards the courtyard where
other museum-goers had also taken refuge, feeling relieved at
least that she would be able to spend a few more hours there,
and that in a bit she would be able to return to the room that
had become so thick with all her worries. Avoiding the noisy
groups of visitors she turned left past Vermeer's *The Soldier and
the Girl,* being careful not to look at Whistler's *The Ocean*
where Maud Franklin was waiting practically naked at the end
of the beach. "Just another *Lady Meux*!" she found herself

thinking despite her dislike of everything that the two men had said.

She sat down on the stone bench in one of the alcoves and began writing in her journal. She had glued the reproduction of *The Peacock Room* to one of the pages, so she decided to enter it, and so she found herself once again in Frederick Leyland's sitting room at 49 Prince's Gate. Thank God the blue rug wasn't there yet. Leyland was still in Liverpool. She could feel the floor creak under her feet; the room was dark, presumably Whistler had finished work for the day. Looking out the window on the left she noticed that the lights in Mrs. Leyland's apartment were on. This time, however, Lady V. did not pass by the fireplace where *La Princesse du Pays de la Porcelaine* hung, nor did she seem too interested in how Whistler's work had progressed that day.

With a determined movement she opened the door and with a few quick steps passed through the dark and slightly damp hallway that connected the two wings of the building. She turned right and found herself in the lobby of Mrs. Leyland's apartment where new furniture had just been delivered. She walked up the marble staircase and was able to distinguish the sounds of a piece of music that, while seeming quite familiar, she could not place even with her wonderful memory. She hesitated in front of the partially open door to the drawing room. She could tell that it was brightly lit, but the music did not come from there and, not hearing any voices, she walked into the room. She stopped, amazed by the giant Venetian mirror that covered half a wall and in which she could immediately see the gramophone, silent while somewhere the melodic line continued.

She studied the room a bit more: it was exactly the room she had always wanted. It was so in touch with her taste and her person that she felt as if she could just sit down in an armchair (something that she immediately did) and time would finally stop, and all these things would belong to her. But she got up, walked across the room to a closed door and bent down shamelessly to look through the keyhole. It was Mrs. Leyland's *boudoir* and it appeared to be empty. Carefully, she opened the door: now the music seemed closer. She could easily distinguish two instruments that seemed to be searching for each other while harmonizing—something that made melody useless, if not downright impossible. They kept *finding* each other at the same harmonic intensity, always the same and yet different. This the ear perceived as music. To her left she discovered Mrs. Leyland's desk with her journal open and the last sentence unfinished.

Under other circumstances, Lady V. would have probably stopped to read it, but now she didn't have time. The Frick was only open until nine and the Japanese photographers may very well have already finished their work in the room where she wished to return as soon as possible. She noticed, thrown on a sofa, the dress that Mrs. Leyland wears in her portrait. It had probably just been brought to her: the fine paper it had been wrapped in was scattered on the floor. Lady V. wanted to try on the dress, but told herself that she had to hurry—she could do it another time. Now that she had decided to enter Mrs.

Leyland's apartment she could do it again any time she wanted, at least until Frederick Leyland came back from Liverpool...

The music was coming from the bedroom, but the door was closed and Lady V. could not see anything through the keyhole. The room was dark: there probably wasn't anyone in there, or maybe Mrs. Leyland was asleep. More than that she could not and did not want to imagine. Returning to the stone bench in the alcove at the Frick, she felt a bit chilly, closed her journal and walked back to the courtyard passing in front of the Vermeer without having the first clue of how much time had passed.

****

As soon as she walked into the room she saw that everyone had crowded in there abandoning the other rooms. Probably because the Japanese photographers were still there talking loudly, laughing and passing out some kind of flyer—probably an advertisement for their millionaire patron's magazine. Trying to avoid the crowd she found herself suddenly in front of *Lady Meux* without having first caught glimpses of it as she approached.

Her shock intensified when she saw the unusual metamorphosis that the painting had undergone. It was just as in the two men's conversation: *Lady Meux* painted in the same posture as *Mrs. Leyland*. Despite feeling like she might faint, Lady V. carefully examined each detail. They were, indeed, just as the short man had predicted a few hours earlier. Still, Lady V.

felt the need to confirm what she saw; she did not, under any circumstances, want to give in to the temptation to imagine God knows what where there was nothing. She wondered if, obsessed by the conversation she had overheard earlier, she might not be dreaming with her eyes open. She thought of asking the old security guard who had known her for many years, but hesitated not knowing how such a question might be phrased. But soon she noticed a couple behind her discussing the portrait in French, and she realized that this would not be necessary:

"Look at those large hips and voluptuous nose. This woman looks like some sort of bird of prey. There is something possessive and also threatening about her … And her gaze, the bit of it that can be seen in profile, looks so empty, though it seems to be trained on something…"

"Oh you poor dear! What a Casanova you are!" the woman answered. "Did this perfidious soothsayer scare you? But I have to admit, you have a point here: she's not exactly displayed in the most advantageous pose. For some reason this Whistler does not compliment her at all—he must have hated her."

It was clear now: Lady V. was not imagining anything. She wasn't sure what had caused the change: whether it was the two gentlemen's conversation or her own insistence on staying there and wishing, perhaps subconsciously, for the change to take place. Not without a trace of meanness, she wondered what would happen if she tried to effect the same change on *The Young American* or *The Fur Jacket*. What would be left after she imposed upon their subject a position that was not "advantageous"? Would something change there too? Had he really made love to Lady Meux? Did he really love Maud Franklin?

She could answer all these questions later, if they even deserved an answer. Something else caught her attention: Mrs. Leyland's portrait which was now attracting dozens of onlookers and from where she could hear all sorts of exclamations and comments. Could it be? If what she had heard a few hours ago had taken its toll on *Lady Meux*—through what means she had no intention of finding out—then logically *Mrs. Leyland* would be…

She did not even want to finish her thought. All she had to do was take a few steps and walk around the growing crowd, something which she managed to do without ever looking at the canvas, even when she was at last standing right in front of it. Once again she covered her eyes with her fingers just as she had done so many years ago at the Tate Gallery, in 1930s London, in front of *Harmony in Gray and Green: Miss Cicely Alexander* when, deciding to completely forget the name of the girl in the painting, she had found none other than herself reflected there in the painting's atmosphere. This time, the ritual was more a necessity than a game. Her fingers were trembling, she was sweating and she found herself in such a tense state that she could hardly stand it. More out of a need to dissipate this tension than of her own will, which now seemed to have evaporated completely, her still trembling fingers started to open.

The light filtered through bringing with it her own face, as if in a mirror. In the forward-facing figure on the canvas, she found herself, this time not just suggested by the composition, but quite explicitly. Of their own volition, her hands slid down as if she were preparing to receive an offering mimicking the position of *Mrs. Leyland*'s hands. People were passing in front of and behind her, but Lady V. remained rooted to that spot for a long time, until she began to wonder if the painting was perhaps watching her instead of the other way around.

The flash of a camera broke her trance. Indignant, she walked toward the old guard to report such an insolent defiance of museum rules: taking photographs with artificial light was strictly forbidden. But the guard calmed her down, explaining that the man was a reporter from the *Village Voice* who had special permission. The old man agreed with Lady V.: the museum should have been closed at five, but the millionaire had made a significant contribution and the *Village Voice* was providing free publicity, so they could afford to flout the rules ... Times were hard, people weren't coming to the museum as in the good old days, the endowment was not enough to finance needed repairs and other costs ... From his extensive and good-natured explanation, Lady V. retained only that the museum would be closing in about ten minutes. It had been an unusually long day...

****

Overnight fall finally arrived: cold, wind, rain ... Anyone else would have taken this as a perfect opportunity to not leave the house; anyone but Lady V. Saturday morning at five to ten she was in front of the museum. She had had a difficult night and the thing that kept nagging at her, both in her dreams and in her bouts of wakefulness, were the hours she spent in that room between the time that the two men left and five o'clock when the Japanese photographers moved in. She could not forgive herself for not having checked the canvases, at least as she was walking out to the courtyard. Now she hadn't the vaguest idea when the metamorphosis had taken place. She may have been right there when it happened and could have seen the process, she thought. Things can't just all of a sudden appear different—or can they?

Of everything that the short man had predicted, only one thing did not happen. The alarm did not go off; no one ran like a sleepwalker toward the painting. Which is not to say that the portrait of *Mrs. Leyland* in its reversed position was not sublime, just that people don't know how to look at paintings: they take everything as a given. The proof was that out of all the people who had been at the museum that night, probably even some art critics, no one had noticed the change. No one!

The museum opened exactly at ten o'clock, but Lady V. did not go directly to the room with the two portraits. She wanted to give herself some more time. Today she would be able to analyze everything much more carefully. She walked through the first room on the right where one could find exquisite old furniture and a few glorious Gainsboroughs. She had brought a large silk scarf with which to cover her head while looking at the portrait of *Mrs. Leyland*. The resemblance was so striking that, no matter how oblivious people were, she did not want to expose herself to any risk.

But as soon as she walked in the room she saw that everything was back to normal: the positions of the women in the paintings appeared just as Whistler had painted them and as they remained on those canvases for more than a century. She walked towards them reproaching herself again for all those hours she had spent in the room the previous day without noticing the paintings and for not being able to remember anything.

Slowly she began feeling better. She took the now useless scarf off her head and walked towards the portrait of *Lady Meux* with something of a malicious smile on her lips. Then she moved on to the portrait of *Mrs. Leyland.* She tried to take it in at once, first the fragments, and then the whole—and she once again found her face in the painting even without yesterday's dramatic posture change.

She left the Frick Museum for the last time, thinking to herself that Frederick Leyland had undoubtedly been in Liverpool far too long. This not just because it had given Whistler a chance to take over the sitting room, changing it into something completely different, or because of the costs he had incurred in letting him do so … Upon her return home, she wrote in the journal that the light that went on in Mrs. Leyland's apartment every night after ten o'clock, when Whistler was done with his work, could perhaps have been the essential element in the irreconcilable conflict between the two peacocks on the wall of *The Peacock Room.*

****

Before ending with Mallarmé's poem, the journal also mentions that for the next few weeks Lady V. had stubbornly tried to acquire an issue of the Japanese art magazine *Senshoku Alphe*, whose name she had learned at the Frick. She had been warned that it would probably cost a lot of money and all the articles would be in Japanese. When she finally managed to get a hold of the magazine, she saw that although the comments were indeed in Japanese, the photographer hadn't missed anything; so much so that even the door that leads to the restroom was reproduced, granted that it is made of sculpted wood. And, of course, there were Whistler's two great paintings, *Lady Meux* and *Mrs. Leyland* as they had appeared that Friday evening. *Mrs. Leyland* especially was accompanied by a commentary of three quarters of a page and Lady V. found herself regretting that it was in Japanese or that over the years she had not managed to learn this language. The reproductions were so true to life that it would have been very easy for her to enter the paintings, though these days Lady V. felt no desire to do so.

For two weeks Lady V. picked up the *Village Voice* without much enthusiasm and found nothing, but on the third week, in the middle of a cold and damp November, she was rewarded with the photograph of herself looking at *Mrs. Leyland*'s reversed portrait under the caption "A Shocking Resemblance" followed by an explanation: "On the evening of… at the Frick Museum, a woman looking at Whistler's famous painting *Mrs. Leyland*. Her twin sister, you might say … Resemblances like this one, however, are not quite as rare as one might expect. Something similar happened just last year at *The Fine Art Museum* of Virginia, in front of the *grouchy* painter Tielsen "Boss" Monroe's famous *The Girl with the Guitar…*" and so on, but Lady V. stopped reading.

****

"Every portrait that is painted with feeling is the artist's portrait, not the model's. The model is more of an accident, a pretext. It is not he who is revealed to us in the painting, but the painter who shows his true self on the colorful canvas," Oscar Wilde wrote.

It does not matter now whether Lady V. transcribed this quote into her journal (no less than four times) because, as some critics claim, it refers to Whistler, or because it provides a sort of key to her whole life: something to liberate her from the tension between *watcher* and *watched*, a theme so common in her journal. After the incident at the Frick she began rereading passages from *The Picture of Dorian Gray*, of which she owned a rare copy with the author's autograph. It was sold, just a few days ago, for a large sum at a Sotheby's auction.

She had cut out her picture from the *Village Voice*. With scissors, she cut out just enough of the description to highlight the shocking resemblance between herself and the changed portrait that only she had been meant to truly *see*, while everyone else had been there purely by coincidence. She was glad that the *Village Voice* made no allusions to the fact that Mrs.

Leyland's stance was reversed. How lucky that people, be they ignorant or snobby, look at paintings as if they were in total, complete isolation! For a long time she ran her fingers across the photograph. Then she placed it on her mother-of-pearl inlay nightstand next to the cast iron lamp that was a reproduction of *The Death of Reason*. On top of the Japanese magazine with detailed descriptions of the paintings at the Frick she placed her copy of *Dorian Gray*. Now all the evidence was there: equally convincing and absolutely useless. She felt the need to put on the dress that Mrs. Leyland had been wearing in the portrait and that she had purchased for a nominal sum at an auction in Manchester thirty years earlier. So dressed, she threw herself on the bed forgetting to turn off the lamp.

****

Rereading Ruskin's stupid commentary from *Fors Clavigera*, Whistler felt the blood rush to his head. It's amazing how people who are so well-educated and have such pretensions to subtlety can sometimes be so insultingly superficial. Swinburne was right, he should just ignore him. Ruskin hadn't even bothered to appear before the court and Whistler had once again exposed himself to the public as superfluous and unsatisfied. His triumph in court left him cold: what could the amused crowd have cared when he answered that painting does not begin or end anywhere and that no genuine painting has an explicitly narrative nature, as both the marginalized Burne-Jones and that opportunist William Powell Frith had jumped to assert. What, after all, is a *whole* and who has the authority to distinguish it from a *fragment*?

"Why doesn't Ruskin count how many hours it took me to finish *Black and Gold: The Falling Rocket*, so that petty bureaucrat, the judge, can divide the two hundred guineas for which I sold it: then we'll know how much a minute of pure art costs!" Whistler thought. "And on top of that, these people are so stupid or so shameless as to speak of *posterity*."

He felt, as he had many times before, that things could just stop at any moment with no warning, only to start again who knows when, if ever. For example this instant, after finishing his bottle of port, after closing his eyes but not falling asleep, thinking of the next day's meeting with Duret. Yes, Duret, the man who, at the very least, would never doubt him. He could ask tomorrow why that is, though who knows if anyone could give him an answer. But in the end, isn't it the sin of doubting that makes time move forward, sometimes crawl, but always bring a new day in which to move from one moment of confusion to the next? Therefore, time could not end now. He finished his bottle of port and threw himself on the bed fully clothed. This time he really closed his eyes.

****

Whistler had finished his bottle of port and thrown himself on his bed. He had obviously been exhausted; he fell asleep right away and she could hear his loud breathing. This was the first time she had been so close to him, and she wanted to run, to disappear as she was, wearing the dress that Mrs. Leyland wears in the painting. It was like all those times crossing the street, especially in Glasgow where cars seemed to come from nowhere and where the color of the stoplight could at best be guessed through the fog, that she had felt herself almost irresistibly drawn toward the vehicle that could strike her at any second.

This time, all she had to do was cross the throw-rug that was next to the bed. She felt something very familiar: despite her nervousness, she felt at ease, as she had in her visits to the house at 49 Prince's Gate in London. That was probably it: Whistler didn't do anything in Mrs. Leyland's apartment but rest. This may also explain that *harmony* she had interpreted as music. Everything seemed so simple and charming and she crossed the carpet with one quick step.

Dressed as she was she laid down on the bed and felt for an instant that commotion, that climax, which had been denied her in all four of her marriages, but which she knew in all its sacred and most hidden details from books and her own instincts. For the first time she thought that her name, *Victory*, could, after all, refer to a triumph: that of recognizing with certainty something that you have never experienced. She jumped when she felt the heat of Whistler's hand stretching to embrace her in his sleep. She tried, in return, to stretch her left hand toward him, with the palm facing upward, damp from an emotion that promised to continue endlessly.

This is how they found her in her apartment on Madison Avenue that morning that would have marked her 79th birthday.

****

In his sleep, Whistler felt the touch of a damp hand and a scent that he had known seemingly forever, though he could not name it. It smelled organic, overpowering, but calming. He told himself that, in fact, things *could* stop at any time: he wondered if this is exactly what had happened as he felt himself surrounded by a feeling of wholeness, unfragmented by fears or doubts. It was like he had found his way back to a place from which he had been missing for a very long time. He would have liked to stay there forever, not asking any questions, not expecting any answers.

But he knew that dreams could not last too long. He raised himself on one elbow, and immediately recognized the girl-woman who was coming towards him with ghostly movements and cold fingers. Her beauty surpassed normal traits: all at once flighty and deeply profound, ageless, enchanting beyond words, forms, or colors. She was the one that he had always been looking for in every woman he knew and, disappointingly, finding only her fragments, here and there. He had loved her ever since childhood, but he had understood, with the passing of time, that he would never meet her. And yet, here she was, and she loved him.

He smiled in his sleep at this thought that would remain and comfort him until the clock at Westminster struck seven times on that otherwise insignificant London morning of the year 1891.

THE CHOICE

A TAINTED PROPERTY

"We're not even talking about whether or not the law is 'good' or 'bad'. The law is—and we profit from it—whatever we manage to prove in court to be legal! And it's been like this all along. I know better than anyone, believe me ... What kind of 'good law' is there beyond this very tangible fact, Bob? I consider you a dear friend, but I swear, you must admit that lately (by which I mean in the last twenty years or so, right, boys?) you've gone a bit off your rocker! Starting with your feeble-minded decision to become a judge. Ladies and gentlemen, the pride of *Moot Court*, the most fearsome of law students, and the valedictorian of the Harvard Law class of '72, Robert 'Bobby' Blair, decided to punish society for all its wickedness and became a judge!"

"Without me you'd all starve," mumbled Bob under his breath, but he was pretty annoyed by Marlon's comments. "And after all," he added, "don't forget: I'm rich enough to allow myself a certain philosophical take on the law. No offense to any of you. This pertains only to Marlon. He's the one who provoked me!"

But all of a sudden and as he spoke, Bob Blair felt a sharp pain in his left ear and a great shudder passed through his body. One damned question seemed to be roaring not only in his head but in the whole room as it would have been there for the past twenty years: *Why the hell did I ever become a judge?*

Marlon wheezed out a laugh (he was a heavy man and had trouble breathing), and grabbed Bob by the shoulders.

"Let's go in. Dinner must be ready, and with a little lobster and *Veuve Cliquot* it'll be much easier to accept your distinctions between 'good law' and 'bad law.' Brad Wilkins, who will be here later, may sort you out in this matter; he wrote an entire treatise after all ... And most importantly, we'll have plenty of time to laugh thoroughly over your adventure with the haunted house where you gave the most *Solomonic* of all possible verdicts ... Ah! If only I'd been that poor Benson's lawyer. I would have made you squirm until you brought me that ghoul for all to see, him and his whole blasted clan. Or perhaps these things don't die? I guess you'd know better Bob. Anyway, the only explanation for why you insist on pursuing such extravagant trifles is the one you just gave yourself: you can afford the luxury, you don't have to work like a dog, like us..."

Bob thought that Marlon Harley had been somewhat put out by the reference to his wealth. After all, he was the descendent of one of the oldest and richest New England families while Marlon had always made his own way in the world. He had worked his way up from a lowly courier for a similarly lowly law firm to the halls of Harvard (where he was a mediocre and overly seasoned student) and then into tax law, where he became involved in all sorts of misappropriations. Nevertheless, he had always walked away with relatively little harm to his reputation, and lots of more or less clean money…

"What verdict?" asked Nick Ashley who had been away from New York for a few months and had just returned from Hollywood where he had served as a legal expert in the famous Disney trial.

"Don't worry." Bob looked bored. "Marlon will give you his version during dinner. It's inevitable…"

Marlon laughed again as if he had been paid a compliment. They passed through to the next room where gasps of surprise replaced the conversation.

The mahogany-paneled dining room of the Westchester mansion had been recently redecorated. The guests were treated to a veritable collection of old European furniture which clashed somewhat with the modern conveniences of the room. The whole was eclectic in its own right, bringing together *Bidermayer* armoires, two *Boulle* screens, *Empire* chairs and an extremely long *Woodsleigh*-style table, not to mention a superb original *Recamier* that Marlon had, most unfortunately, covered in gold-leaf. The farthest wall of the room was made entirely of green glass and looked onto the pool, also glass-enclosed. The sconces on the walls had been replaced by candelabras holding real beeswax candles and under each one stood a valet dressed in a style that brought to mind old English TV shows.

"Do they also sing?" asked Phil McCormick sarcastically. "You seem to have brought the entire cast of the Metropolitan here. Do you pay them by the hour…?"

"Very funny," answered an irritated Marlon.

"I swear, you must be taking money from the Mafia," continued McCormick grabbing him by the collar and stumbling slightly.

"And you could stand to change your 'mouthwash'," answered Marlon sharply. "What the hell? You've started this again?"

Phil McCormick bit his lip, stumbled a bit more, then made a dismissive gesture with his hand and followed the others into the room. He was a very astute lawyer but a sensitive person before that. Perhaps it was exactly this last quality combined with his naturally acerbic personality and his radical tendencies that had driven him to alcoholism and to the edges of the stuffy society of the Harvard Law class of '72. For a while he had stopped practicing altogether and had gone through detox. Some gossips maintained that he hadn't won a case in two years. The same well-intentioned sources passed around rumors that even the tux that he occasionally wore, for example to Marlon's party, he had bought for almost nothing from *Katharsis*, the Greek dry cleaner in Astoria where one could often buy used clothes, sometimes of the highest quality.

No more than two hours had passed when, after the champagne, caviar, lobster, quail, and *osso bucco*, all washed down with a 1982 *Saint-Emillion* as is proper, Marlon's booming voice broke up the chatter and laughter that had sprung up among the various little cliques.

"*Caveat emptor*! That's all that could be said about the case at hand. It is the buyer's responsibility to thoroughly research the property he is about to purchase! Beyond this, and once the contract is signed, there can be no doubt about the deal. Unless of course you have the bad luck to come before the Honorable Judge Blair, who, from the heights of his position which, might I add, is paid for with taxes that take the food out of the mouths of orphans and widows, will judge otherwise and determine that this sacred principle is in fact 'bad law'. Can you believe that!? While all our affairs are picked through with a fine-toothed comb..."

"And some of us," hiccupped McCormick, "seem also to have been born under a lucky star such that we do not have to pay taxes at all. Not only that, but we also get a refund from the State and from the Feds ... How long has it been since you've paid taxes, Marlon?"

"That's because I have a good lawyer, Phil," Marlon shot back, "not a looser like yourself. But anyway, that's another story. So ... Someone sells a house in Nyack and after some time the buyer, a certain Collins, sues the former owner claiming a breach of contract and demanding damages, insisting that the house is haunted and that Benson, the former owner, knew about all of this before the sale ... Felonies, malicious with-holding of information, psychological trauma—Bob swallows all this guilelessly; moreover, in the ruling he wrote (I have a fresh copy in my drawer, boys!), he maintains that Collins is entitled to damages, and Benson is guilty of having sold a 'karmically tainted property', as if such a thing even existed! A thousand thanks, your Honor, for adding yet another idiocy to our already too wooly judicial vocabulary: 'a tainted property' and, in the case before us, no more and no less than 'kar...', 'ker...', 'karmically' so. Between the drink and my indignation I can't even pronounce it!"

"You can't pronounce the word, not because of the drink or because of your indignation," Phil said. "But because you are singularly ignorant. You don't know where it comes from: *karma. Karma—karmic.* It's an Indian concept having to do with transmigration; that is, of course, if one recognizes the existence of reincarnation or a sort of evolution of the soul, exactly that invisible core that you are missing. I think that's what Bob was referring to, probably in more general terms, in his ruling about which, after all, we know nothing. Perhaps it would be best if you let him speak!"

"And I can answer you that in my house I know best who has something to say and when he should say it! As for you, in general, you would be well served to just drink and shut up: two things you are extremely good at!"

This was a low blow: about Phil's drinking problem we have already spoken, and the mention of shutting up alluded to a panic attack he had had in court several years earlier when, having to give closing arguments in a case that was as good as his, he suddenly found himself unable to swallow, choked, then cleared his throat a few times, but was ultimately unable to utter a sound though his lips moved desperately in search of the words.

"I would like to disagree here," interrupted Nick Ashley. "Blair is not the one who coined the terms 'tainted' or 'karmic'. I'll refer you to *Green v. Kingston.* In 1983..."

"Yes, of course," Marlon cut him off. "But that was in California! Fine for them! What is the law in California? Those people get too much sun; they'd be capable of seeing ghosts on the street in plain daylight. And the judges would buy anything, that's how bored they are by all the bureaucratic stupidity they deal with. But here, in the glorious state of New York in 1997, what could a 'tainted property' mean legally? Have you ever seen one?"

"Without a doubt," smirked McCormick. "But I suppose you might be too close to it to have the proper perspective on the situation! And what I'm referring to is deeply 'karmic', if you catch my drift, you old charlatan..."

"You'd do well to take another double *Jack Daniels*, for some ... perspective! Then, if you still have your voice, you can tell us about all the rabbits, bugs, rats and other creatures that we can't see because of our ... lack of perspective!"

Blair made an instinctual gesture as if to say something, but McCormick grabbed him firmly by the arm.

"Let him be, Bob. I'm used to his slurs."

CAVEAT SPIRITUS!

Things calmed down a bit after the arrival of Brad Wilkins, a well-respected professor who, despite being the same age as most of them (with the exception of course of Marlon Harley) looked much older, perhaps because of his hair, which had begun to gray when he was still in college. He had indeed written a treatise about the nature of law, now in its fourth revised edition, which was considered fundamental reading in both the judicial and academic fields and which had all the features of a book that is appreciated by almost everyone: solidly documented, articulately written, lacking all jargon but also any original or controversial ideas. Since the first chapter referred to the difference between "good law" and "bad law," and as Marlon never read more than the first thirty or forty pages of any book, for him Wilkins' treatise was simply "the book about good law and bad law."

"Ah!" Marlon exclaimed, "Our dear scholar, you couldn't have come at a better time! Today, the Honorable Judge Blair, our dear friend Bobby, has written one of the most disturbing opinions known to contemporary jurisprudence. Let us thank him, firstly, for lighting our way in such a hazy area, and then let him get his well deserved punishment from you! Bobby has declared no more and no less than that the principle of *caveat emptor* is 'bad law'! Dear Wilkins, I will let you deal with him now!"

The audience found this oration quite amusing, but this did not incite Brad Wilkins to jump down his supposed adversary's throat. Anyone who knew him would have realized he was not the type.

"In principle, Marlon, I consider *caveat emptor* to be 'good law,' but only in the general spirit of what distinguishes 'good law' from 'bad law.' I don't know any of the implications of Blair's case. It's possible that in that instance it wasn't 'good law'; everything depends on the circumstances..."

Marlon was obviously unhappy with his friend's perform-
ance and hastened to add, "Well if it's a question of circumstances, then our friend is really in trouble: imagine two parties
who, under no duress, sign a contract. The contracted property is then sold, the money changes hands, and after more than
a year the buyer sues the former owner, demands that the contract be voided, his money back and damages on top of it!
Incidentally, my friend, this is the third time when our honorable Blair has indulged himself in such extravagances ... I swear
it's like he goes looking for these lunatics!"

Bob felt a sudden stabbing lucidity he could not explain
and realized for a moment that Marlon was, in his own way,
right. It rather felt that this sort of case came looking for him,
not the other way around...

"Anyway," said Wilkins, "these cases are not so incredibly
uncommon. If the property had undisclosed faults (like a ter-
mite infestation which can't be seen right away) and the owner
intentionally failed to warn the buyer, then *caveat emptor* certainly could not be 'good law'."

"Thank you, Brad," replied Blair distractedly, though it
seemed that his mind was not there at all, but rather on: *Why
the hell did I ever become a judge?*

"Except that the 'termites' in this case, dear Professor
Wilkins, are no more and no less than ghosts, phantoms,
ghouls or whatever you want to call them! And Blair declares
the house 'karmic property' and throws out the defense's case,
which is based on the very reasonable principle of *caveat emptor*. Now what do you have to say?"

"Bob, you don't actually believe in ghosts!" exclaimed Brad Wilkins instinctively, though he immediately regretted having played into Harley's game.

"Quiet!" shouted Marlon. "This is a very solemn moment: you will now hear something unheard of! We will see now in whose hands the state places the power to dole out justice. So, Bob, do you believe in ghosts or not?"

Blair felt again that stabbing pain behind his left eye, and also a premonition of nausea, together with the unanswered question: *Why the hell did I ever become a judge?*

"This is not a question of what I do or do not believe! I declared *caveat emptor* 'bad law' because that crook, Benson, had already made a tidy sum by selling his ghost stories to television ... Then along comes Collins, a stranger from Nebraska, no one tells him about any of this, he buys the house and then he starts having problems..."

"And what kind of problems, may I ask?" pipes up Marlon.

"What does it matter? The contract was based on a fraud, a lie, don't you get it? That's why I disregarded *caveat emptor*: it didn't apply in this case. And furthermore, Harley, you're not going to make me say more than that, no matter what you may think!"

"Big deal, you and your contract!" interjected Marlon clearly losing ground.

"Don't be like that," intervened Nick Ashley. "Any contract has its unwritten rules, some sort of moral guarantee, be it God, or the law, or any other valid principle ... Isn't that so, Brad?"

"Of course there are 'unwritten rules', Nick dear; that's a very nice way of putting it. Roscoe Pound, on whose writing I base many of my distinctions between 'good law' and 'bad law', would have liked it very much. On the other hand, how could we know if there is a divine guarantee behind every contract without committing Lucifer's sin. What could God want other than that the contract be honest, based on good faith and rationalism..."

"Aha! You said rationalism!" Marlon shouted. "Well how could you reconcile rationalism and general good sense with believing in ghosts, ghouls, reincarnations and all the other chimeras that Blair, from his tenuous position, generously accords to Collins along with a substantial amount of money? Termites, OK! Everyone can see them, and if the buyer was negligent too bad for him; he'll have to suffer the consequences. *Caveat emptor* as we've already said. But when it comes to ghosts, where is the proof?"

Blum, Harrison, and Lambert, tax attorneys like Marlon, agreed enthusiastically much to his satisfaction. He felt himself regaining the ground he had lost earlier in the argument.

"There are different kinds of proof, Marlon," answered a thoughtful Wilkins. "In my book, I specifically mention so called 'properties with psychological traumas' as an exception to *caveat emptor* being 'good law'. This does not mean of course that the house itself has psychological traumas, which would be absurd, but that different individuals may have an extremely strong and perfectly credible emotional reaction provoked by certain circumstances ... For example, a house that belonged to a suicide, or to a..."

"You crook!" cackled McCormick. "The sudden nausea you feel when stepping over the threshold is a form of proof!"

"No one is forcing you to buy my house Phil; not that you'd even have the money!" replied the now hoarse Marlon, making it clear that this situation could quickly degenerate into something horrid.

In the general chaos, Brad Wilkins tried to maintain some sort of thread to the conversation. "What I'm trying to say is that 'ghosts', whether they exist or not, can severely impact the well-being of a family who buys a house known for ... for such things ... And in a pluralistic society such as ours, where we allow for a multitude of religious beliefs, it's easy to make such a case, even in a court of law, as long as, let's say, the effects of the psychological trauma are obvious ... Bob would know better if this was the case when he decided to declare *caveat emptor* 'bad law'."

"In fact I did have such proof, exactly as you explained it, Brad!" said Blair all of a sudden. "Thank you for trying to contradict, at least partially, the theory you developed in your treatise, but I don't need you to make any concessions here. The Collins' suffered, if you will, a true psychological assault in that house, and I myself was beset by shudders and felt faint upon entering."

A heavy silence fell over the room. Marlon triumphantly refilled his glass without uttering another word, downed its entire contents, and, satisfied, burped loudly.

"Maybe you were suffering from indigestion," Nick Ashley

suggested amicably, rather taken aback by how easily Blair had given in to Harley.

"Indigestion? Not a chance!" Mumbled McCormick swaying but refusing to stop talking. "I myself have felt quite ill since I stepped in this house; I find the food revolting..."

"Not the drink though," remarked Lambert, Harley's right hand man.

"Nooo! Of course not!" Phil said in a sing-song. "Drink is *spiritus*, it can't be 'tainted'! As for everything else, I feel Belial's breath emanating from all the walls, the furniture, the paneling..."

"Who or what the hell is this *Belial* you're talking about? Come, if you stop talking I'll order you your own bottle of that *Belial*, no matter how much it costs me," said Marlon annoyed that everyone had laid down their forks as if they had no intention of tasting anything more. "What a jester you are..."

"Oh, God! How horribly and incurably ignorant can this man be?" exclaimed Phil McCormick taking another sip from his glass of bourbon.

"And you're a drunk!" came Harley's irritated reply.

"Yes, but I'll be clean and sober in the morning. For you there's no cure."

The others pulled the two apart, because they had come closer and closer to each other and were posturing like a pair of roosters spoiling for a fight. Robert Blair took McCormick aside.

"Phil, it would be best if you went home. I'll call you tomorrow. I'm sure you're right: for the past two hours I too have been feeling this sharp pain here and there in my head and a sort of nausea. Let Harley be..."

"What are you two plotting over there?" asked Marlon much more calmly, ready to move past the incident that threatened to spoil the party.

"We aren't plotting anything, Harley!" McCormick spat through his teeth. "Only Satan plots ... As for the rest of you, don't forget: *Caveat Spiritus! Caveat Spiritus! Caveat Spiritus!*

AN ASIDE

As soon as Phil McCormick left the room, a breeze that seemed to come out of nowhere blew out all the candles and the guests seated around the table began showing signs of unease. Their chatter covered the echo of these last words that now seemed, more than anything else, like a warning or a threat.

Back when Bob Blair was studying law at Harvard, Carol Whitehead had been a charming girl. She attended the journalism school there, permitting herself to take just a course or two a year, as she was much more interested in the company of the other brilliant students at the celebrated university than in earning a degree. Her name had, however, appeared in a few magazines even as early as her undergraduate years. Having come from a wealthy family, she did not trouble herself too much to finish her Master's despite her indisputable intelligence and talent. Perhaps she prolonged her stay at the pleasant Cambridge Campus exactly because of the constraints of growing up in a family where the only thing she lacked was contact with the real world.

Bob had fallen in love with her without reserve, with all the passion of a young man who had always been studious and who came from a family that, like Carol's, could offer him everything except genuine emotions. They married against their parents' will. The older generations of both families felt (out of decency or indifference, not that it matters!) that such a step should be undertaken only after they had finished their studies, especially since neither of the "children" had been taught much about sex, love, or marriage at home.

But Carol was much more advanced in these matters and in the end she determined the outcome of the whole story by getting pregnant and insisting that she would keep the child in spite of any obstacles. The families gave in for obvious reasons and the result, Daniel R. Blair, was now studying law at Berkeley with the intention of becoming a judge, something that Bob found extremely irritating.

He felt closer to Myra, born six years later and a student at Vassar, who intended to get a degree in Creative Writing from Columbia after graduation. She was a delicate and sickly child, or perhaps just overly sensitive and nervous, who had begun writing poetry at the age of four.

As for Carol, it seems that after her exceptional act of will which had at once united the couple and defied their conservative families all of her spirit and will to live had withered. She never finished her studies and spent the rest of her life in the shadow of the great Judge Robert Blair, the valedictorian of the Harvard Law class of '72.

In the semi-darkness of the room and more out of boredom than anything else, Bob reviewed the incomprehensible circumstances that had caused a love story so far removed from any materialism to degenerate into a conventional marriage that still existed (if only on paper) simply because of his insistence. She had accepted, after countless discussions, that for the children's sake they would never divorce. Bob distinctly remembered the day when Carol, in the middle of one of those interminable fits of crying, had confessed that there was someone else in her life.

"How common and painful," he thought at the time, and didn't even bother, at least out of curiosity, to ask who. Instead, Carol herself tossed him a videotape and went off to bed stuffed with a double dose of valium. For months afterwards they did not speak except when strictly necessary while he wondered if she knew that he had never watched the tape and she could not care less about what he thought.

After Phil McCormick's departure, Blair was the only one who did not rise from the comfortable armchair in which he was seated. The others, agitated by the prolonged darkness, milled around waiting for something to break the tension.

This something was to come soon enough. From the direction of the glass wall that separated the room from the covered pool small lights like fireflies advanced in a kind of stylized dance while a lascivious sort of music filled the room. One by one, a dozen young women, scantily clad, carrying colored lanterns, and wearing professional smiles entered the room and gathered around Marlon who presided over the whole assemblage from his massive throne. The valets entered from the other direction carrying trays of liquors and open boxes of cigars and cigarettes...

"Boys, I think we're done discussing theory for tonight!" exclaimed Harley very pleased by the effect the scene produced. "You have here all the elements for total relaxation: cigarettes (I don't need to tell you what kind), drinks of the highest quality, and these lovely belly-dancers capable of driving away any ghost, real or unreal—not that it matters now. We'll draw their panties from a hat, so that each of them will participate in a 'trial' that will show you once and for all what I think is 'good law'. Hurry up! They're all eager for the subtleties of your minds and especially for the strength of your virtues, which I am sure you will demonstrate with their skilled help until tomorrow morning!"

And sure enough no sooner had he finished talking than a large golden vessel filled with panties of different colors, each bearing a number, appeared next to him.

"Come Bobby! Stop sitting there sulking. Come quickly and draw a number and you'll soon forget about ghosts and obsessions. Come if you don't want to end up with God knows what left-over, and I swear, you wouldn't have the right to any *caveat emptor* this time!"

The others, particularly the contingent of business lawyers, had immediately followed the orders of their host. Bob Blair, however, did not get up from his armchair and said to Marlon who had come up to him and had placed his arm protectively around the shoulders, "Harley, I hope you realize that you are a very sick individual!"

Blair's reply had been loud enough for all to hear, and Marlon carried on in his dinner theater tone, "Yes, yes, yes, yes! Finally you've hit the nail on the head: I am sick, very sick. Hey girls, come here and cure this terrible illness I suffer from. Ah! I have a feeling I'll be quite healthy by the end of the night." With that he grabbed two of the young girls around the waist while they, giddy from the drink and Marlon's special cigarettes, began undressing him.

Now enlivened by the sounds of the couples that, once formed, ran to the pool or found themselves the most comfortable spots among the deep armchairs by the wall, the room once again sank into darkness and only the colored lamps of the "belly-dancers" continued to bounce around for a while.

Blair realized that the warm arms of a creature whose face he could not see very well had encircled him. Before he even noticed what was going on, she had settled herself almost weightlessly on his knee. The way she raked her fingers on the back of his neck almost mechanically made him jump and annoyed him, and the perfumed breath gliding across his cheek towards his ear convinced him to stand up immediately. But he did not do it, because he felt something cold against the side of his chin and made out the outline of a large crucifix hanging around the girl's neck. She was not naked like all the others— she had on a pair of silk harem pants and a thin kimono. She was without a doubt very young and Bob suddenly felt like he was holding the sister that he had never had...

He gave up all attempts to get up. To the girl he whispered, "Listen... it's not what you think; all I want is ... Don't move and if you're cold I can give you my coat ... Stay here; nothing's going to happen between us ... What's your name?"

"Amy," replied the girl also whispering. "You can call me Amy. Don't worry; I won't do anything to you either ... I'm not very good at these things anyway ... If you want I can sit next to you; the chair's big enough especially since I'm missing a rib. I was born that way," she said, smiling in a way that made Bob feel extremely calm.

IN THE CLEARING AT ENGLEWOOD

Bob had eventually watched the tape a few months or perhaps almost a year later—he couldn't even remember now. He was never really able to shake the surprise of discovering that his wife had been living with Meredith Sommers, the shrink he himself had sent her to when Carol's breakdowns became much too frequent. And so he had never managed, in almost ten years, to discuss it with her. All he felt was a strong sense of pity and incredible guilt which, in addition to a crippling sense of powerlessness, stayed with him for the rest of his life. Sometimes he felt that from now on his and Carol's lives ran along two parallel tunnels that never met and whose walls were impenetrable. The children had grown; he couldn't even remember exactly how or who they had become with the exception of a few scattered pleasant memories mostly related to Myra. Protected by his wealth, he hadn't bothered to do anything beyond the absolute minimum for a lawman with an impressive education and an equally impressive intelligence: he had written two books of essays on legal matters and had reached the Supreme Court of New York State. All these without distinguishing himself in any way, with the possible exception of the cases dealing with properties touched by inexplicable elements that had been coming to him in the past few years and in which, as Marlon had maliciously emphasized, he almost always ruled for the plaintiff. Everyone knew that he based his judgement on whatever he felt when visiting the house in question—nausea, dizziness, terrible migraines—and if his name were not *Blair* he might very well have been disrobed for such weaknesses which, though not explicitly mentioned in his official opinions, always made him find the necessary elements to obtain the desired verdict in court.

"Perhaps that drunkard McCormick was right," thought Bob through the fog that had enveloped him while sitting there in the armchair. "What could all these things mean other than some desperate *Caveat Spiritus*?" Otherwise he felt useless, almost dead, good for nothing and no one, and the question that had haunted him throughout the night, *Why the hell had he become a judge?* kept whirling around in his head like a trapped moth.

"Maybe I am dead," he mumbled while trying to come back

to life. He felt cold and went to pull his coat over his shoulder, but remembered that he had given it to Amy and she had almost certainly fallen asleep and slid out of his arms. He could hear her breathing. Beyond this everything seemed desolate. It must have been late, probably almost morning, and Marlon's licentious circle must have found refuge in the numerous bedrooms. It would be best if he woke the girl, found her something more appropriate to wear, called her a cab, and sent her home.

Trying to get out of the armchair, he realized that in fact he had been sitting on something hard, uncomfortable, and leaning against a tree. He stood up and almost fell tripping over a shield in hard leather that felt rough and damp. Torches began to glow from the direction of the pool and Bob noticed an unusual amount of activity around a barrel clearly outlined in the light cast by the torches. On the barrel sat a gigantic, tattooed man giving orders left and right.

Looking down, Bob realized he was wearing a sort of long tunic under a loose vest that was much too large for his build and had braid lined buttonholes. Over all this, a heavy medallion hung around his neck hampering his movements. He did not try too hard to understand what had happened, knowing Marlon to be capable of all sorts of tricks and spectacles, but was somewhat perturbed when passing his hand across his cheek he found it covered with a heavy beard. As daylight began to spread slowly from the direction of the pool, he realized that he was in fact at the edge of a clearing completely surrounded by trees. He could now see clearly all the way to the middle of the clearing where Marlon sat on a barrel covered in multicolored tattoos that spread even onto his eyelids while a group of penitents advanced toward him moaning while whipping their backs with knotted ropes.

"Who are you?" Marlon asked in a thundering voice as he sat with his arms crossed across his chest like a sphinx.

"I am the Son," whimpered the first penitent briefly pausing in his self-flagellation.

"Where are you going?"

"I am returning to my Father who has sent me to suffer in this dark world from which I now return, for He is the Eternal One and I am his only Son and since He is eternal and I am of His seed I now return to my rightful place!"

"You shall not pass," howled the man who, in Blair's eyes, so resembled Marlon, "because you are either a liar and not of the Eternal Father, or you insult the Father whose seed was never sown."

"Sire! Sire! Sire!" murmured the penitent as he turned back and resumed his self-flagellation with an air of resignation.

Stunned, Bob kept listening to this dialog when he felt the girl move next to him. "Amy, what's going on here?" he asked instinctively, though how the girl could have known any more than he did having been asleep the entire time.

"Shush," she replied bringing a finger to her lips, "don't move and be quiet!"

Bob noticed that all the penitents were treated in more or less the same manner: after an inquisition of varying length, each was sent back. Towards the end of the ceremony, one of them especially caught his attention for the way he kept covering his face, pulling the hood of his cloak over his cheek after every answer, and the decisive way in which he approached his interlocutor.

"I am the Son and I come from the Father who was before everything and everyone and will be onto eternity."

"If that were true," replied Marlon, "then you would not be sundered from the Father, yet you are sundered from Him or you would not be standing in front of me!"

"And I will tell you," answered the penitent uncovering just enough of his face for his words to be heard, "that I am both from the Father and sundered from Him as He wanted me to come down with all the descendents of Achamoth through whom He bore Sophia without coupling but only with the Law that would let her bear!"

"You are more wretched than everyone here," cried the tattooed Marlon, "because you mix up the Father with your own genesis which is transient!"

"And I tell you, Sire of all Sires, that I am going to my Father who ordered the world so that, *when I do not know how to die, I may look for Him who gave us the Law.* This is how I return to the place I came from and from where I am in no way sundered as you are for having been born out of Achamoth and sin. And for proof I call upon the undying knowledge that is the Father who gave the Law to Achamoth..."

As he spoke these words, a long chant of *"Gnosis! Oh, Gnosis!"* rose from all directions and Blair noticed that there were perhaps hundreds of men and women in the clearing kneeling as if for a liturgy and they had begun singing a series of strange, polyphonic hymns half in English and half in Latin of which he could distinguish only one phrase that went something like: "Glory be to you, Adam, Adam Christ, our Savior and the confessor to Your Father, glory be to You!"

All this time Marlon, still on top of the barrel, was thrashing about foaming at the mouth and cursing his own mother until he was taken away by two similarly tattooed men with rings in their ears.

The hymns continued for a while and the penitent removed his hood, revealing the face of an adolescent, almost a child, with long, blond locks. A face that could just as easily belong to a boy or a girl. Then he raised his arms; the marks of the nails were clearly visible in his palms, and when he removed his clothing he revealed a bloody stain underneath his left rib.

"Amy! Amy!" shouted Robert Blair trying to catch the girl who had wandered away from him. All he felt, however, was the cold touch of the crucifix and the chain on which it hung from the girl's neck.

"Calm down," she replied, annoyed. "Shut up and watch if you're here anyway. And stop calling me Amy ... What kind of name is that?"

"You're the one who told me that's your name," answered Bob, now annoyed in turn.

"Not so loud," the girl scolded him, "or the guard will hear you!"

SOROR MYSTICA[5]

In the meantime the clearing had once again come to life, but now an altar appeared where the barrel had stood, or perhaps someone had just covered the barrel with thick brocade. The smell of the frankincense burning in the censers that the participants swung around reached Bob all the way at the edge of the clearing where he and the girl were hiding.

Soon a priest appeared, knelt before the altar, and remained so, as if in a trance, for minutes on end. Meanwhile, voices could be heard singing from all directions and Bob realized that they were not singing *Gloria in Excelsis Deo* or any other hymn that he recognized, but rather a strange blend of verses in Greek and broken Latin which would have been completely unintelligible to him were it not for a verse that kept recurring and which spoke of *Aurora Consurgens*...

Blair was familiar with the typical mass, but could not tell which sect was celebrating its mystery here and, as usual when something captivated his attention, he forgot completely about Amy and Marlon's party.

The priest stood and kissed the brocade that was draped over the barrel where, instead of the usual tabernacle holding the sacred elements of the Transubstantiation, an ovoid rock rested on a miniature pedestal. In the prayer that he directed to the altar the priest repeated the word *summa* several times instead of the typical *Kyrie*, explicitly invoking God as the inspiration of the sacred science and Jesus as the philosopher's

[5] Mystical sister.

stone, *lapis*. The prayer was accompanied by a chorus of which Bob, once again, understood nothing except that Adam was the same as Jesus. The Gospel reading was from Luke 10:42, as Bob later confirmed, and underlined the two paths to salvation: "Mary hath chosen that good part, which shall not be taken away from her."

With these words, the silhouette of a woman wearing a green silk veil appeared to the right of the altar while the choir intoned an unspeakably beautiful hymn and sang with great feeling: *Ave praeclara maris stella!*[6] Blair was disturbed by the appearance of the woman—there was something very familiar about her—but only when she reached the circle of light cast around the altar by the torches did he realize what it was and exclaimed: "Botticelli's *Spring*!"

"Shush," Amy said. "That's the emerald queen. Wherever she passes everything turns green and comes to life!"

Bob was fascinated by this real life reproduction of Botticelli's painting in the middle of the extremely complicated ritual, especially now that the priest, instead of moving on to the *Credo* that would have normally followed, launched into a strange prayer, spoken half in Latin and half in English. He drew an analogy between the way in which Christ, through His chaste conception, saved the world by dying for its sins and the way that the sacred arts or sciences, through their transgressions, would uncover the philosopher's stone which would ennoble and save imperfect matter. For the success of the latter, he invoked the help of God, here named the 'sacred fire'. He

[6] Hail, most splendid Star of the Sea!

referred once again to the Gospel according to Luke, stressing the words *but one thing is needful,* then turned to the altar and murmured: *Fundamentum vero artis est corporum solutio!*[7]

Blair could understand the following surprising invocation, which the priest delivered with his arms wide open and his eyes trained to the sky, only because unlike most of his colleagues, he had studied both Roman law and Latin for several years:

Similiter per hanc Artem cognoverunt et judicaverunt antiqui Philosophi hujus artis, virginem debere concipere et parere quia apud eos hic lapis concipit et impregnatus a se ipso, et parit se ipsum: unde est conceptio similis conceptioni virginis, quae absque viro concipit.[8]

He lost track of the words, but noticed that the figure that so resembled Botticelli's *Spring* bowed before the priest who blessed her by making the sign of the cross over her. Then she disappeared in the direction from which she had come.

"Anne, Anne!" Bob heard some voices behind him, "Hurry! It's your turn!"

The girl slinked away through the trees, but Blair was, by this point, much too caught up in the developments of this strange ceremony to pay any attention to her disappearance. He did, however briefly, note that they had called her Anne and not Amy.

[7] The foundation of art is the dissolution of the bodies.

[8] Likewise through this art the ancient philosophers of this art knew and determined that a virgin had to conceive and give birth because it is their belief that this stone conceives itself and is impregnated by itself and gives birth to itself: whence the conception is similar to the virgin's conception who conceived without a man.

He was shocked by the way that all these fundamental Christian mysteries were reinterpreted in a *material* context. Despite his intelligence and extensive cultural knowledge, he could not make sense of the spectacle in its entirety. He likened it to an allegory. Clearly the religious service he was now witnessing was closely linked to the earlier interrogations of the penitents conducted by the nobleman who resembled Marlon. The Transubstantiation, thought Bob, could not be far off, but now the priest, instead of invoking the Holy Trinity, said:

Sic mundus creatus est.

Itaque vocatus sum Hermes Trismegistus, habens tres partes Philosophiae totius mundi.

Completum est quod dixi de operatione Solis[9]

Blair did not have much time to reflect upon the bizarre invocation of Hermes Trismegistus in a Christian liturgy because the priest had already turned back to the altar while the choir, which seemed to be comprised of at least one hundred male and female voices, began a new hymn: *Veni, Soror Mystica!*[10]

Bob looked around and only then realized that Amy had gone, remembered that she had been called, and felt once again, clearly and painfully, the lack of something that he had never really possessed, like a helpless craving that was being stoked by the melody of the invocation.

The priest turned with his arms upraised as Amy descend-

[9] For this reason I was named Hermes the Thrice-Greatest since I possess the three parts of the philosophy of the whole world. What I said about the working of the Sun came to pass.

[10] Come, you mystical sister!

ed from a nearby tree, shrouded in a glow that came neither from the torches nor from the gigantic candle burning on the altar. It was like an emanation of light and Bob wanted to approach her, but the girl's gaze paralyzed him. *Amaradaminda! Amaradaminda! Amaradaminda!* He could hear voices intoning from all directions. All of a sudden he felt an inner quiet as he had not felt in a very long time, like the dream state of his earliest childhood which he could just barely remember.

"*Good day and good praise, goodwife!*" murmured the choir, and she replied:

"*If I were to be descending*
I might take away your strife
And your knowledge of true longing!"

Blair felt the salty taste in his mouth first and only then thought to brush away the tears that had been flowing into his beard (the new beard that he could barely get used to but which he must nonetheless accept). The look in Amy's eyes when she spoke these verses pierced him deeply, and for the first time he could not help but think that everything that had happened there that night was meant for *him and him only*. This thought so repelled him that he decided to leave the clearing immediately.

He realized that he would probably have to pass through the length of Harley's eclectic salon where God only knows what orgy had just ended or was about to end. The thought that he might be stopped and asked to explain the beard or the strange attire he was wearing (and for which, deep down, he still held Marlon somehow responsible) filled him with a mixed sense of nausea and powerlessness. He reminded himself that he had to get out of there, though part of him was curious to see the end of such a theatrical mass, especially the way in which the priest would eventually resolve the Transubstantiation.

Of all this however, the thing that seemed most urgent was the feeling that everything concerned him and his person and was somehow tied to the sister he had never had. Then, as he fearlessly passed through the room where various couples whispered indistinctly and the occasional laugh or sob cut like a knife through the silence, Bob asked himself one last time: *Why the hell had he ever become a judge?*

ENGLEWOOD, 1692

As he walked out he could hear a voice behind him saying, "Did you see that? Maybe Phil and Blair were right, there are ghosts here ... Marlon, what is this specter ... look, it looks like it's walking on air. Go away, get out of here!" Marlon replied in a hoarse voice presumably having just woken, "Yes, my dear, ghosts, exactly. Let's play a little more ... at you know what ... so we can see them better."

The forest proved to be less dense than he had first imagined. It was more like a curtain of trees that ended in a narrow, muddy path (it had rained recently). Bob passed through and managed the walk fairly well by carefully hopping from one stone to another in the tall boots that had appeared on his feet out of nowhere just like the beard and everything else. What slowed him down most was the heavy medallion hanging from his neck which he occasionally turned so it hung at his back without tripping him up. The road led to a small village whose humble dwellings were just beginning to peek out in the tentative light of dawn.

The church could be seen through all the tombstones in the adjoining cemetery, but Bob realized that it was taking him much longer than he had imagined to reach it. He was tired and wanted to rest but was still torn between the impulse to raise his hand and hail a cab as he would in his normal life in New York, and this strange situation of looking for shelter somewhere. In the end he just kept going.

As he reached the house, a rooster began announcing the arrival of morning over this rather depressing landscape punctuated by a few sleepy hens in the yard and the desperate bleating of several goats asking for their breakfast, an indication that their master was not an early riser. Blair walked around the church and up to the tiny adjoining cottage which seemed completely abandoned except for a tiny wisp of smoke rising placidly from the chimney. He knocked on the rough wooden door using his fist and, after a time, he heard a hoarse voice approaching.

"Are you the minister?" asked Blair seemingly unable to reconcile in his head the image of a minister with that of the tall, old man with tangled greasy hair and a dirty night shirt who opened the door.

"Yes, I am," mumbled the minister, "*Dominus vobiscum* and all that other stuff," he added as if dazed. "This isn't the best time for confession, but otherwise all strangers are welcome here ... well, at least as welcome as you can be at the abode of a poor country minister. Hard times," he mumbled as he headed back toward the unmade bed, "and I have gout too. I should retire somewhere where it's sunny. This humidity is horrible for me. I've written a short note asking for a transfer, but it seems that here, in Englewood, Massachusetts, *anno Domini* 1692, I am the only one who is not allowed to abandon his post. The Archbishop won't even hear of it."

Bob looked carefully around the foul-smelling chamber and finally decided to sit on an uncomfortable three-legged stool that was the only place a sane person would have chosen to sit in that room. The soles of his feet tingled from all the walking he had done, so that even being perched on this stool was a somewhat comforting change.

"Let me make you some tea," said the old man heading towards the dirty hearth where brown bugs clambered around at will.

The thought of touching the greasy mug, that the minister produced, made Blair feel nauseous.

"Never mind the tea. Thank you!" he said. "I'd rather know what's going on in the clearing in the woods."

The minister turned around with wide eyes, put the cup down, wiped his wet hands on the dirty shirt and sat down on the bed, his joints creaking audibly.

"Were you there?" he asked. "Of course you were, otherwise you wouldn't be asking me. I don't know who you are, but you seem to be an educated man. I have nothing to do with it, but I can tell you that this isn't going to end well," he added, crossing himself theatrically.

"How many ministers are in this town?" asked Bob.

"In Englewood?" asked the man in a distracted tone. "Well, just one. How many did you think? And that one just so happens to be me."

"What about the one in the clearing? What kind of sect conducts its services there?"

The minister waved his hand dismissively, "There's no sect. It's the sheriff's idea. He wants to keep all the malcontents together. He says it'll be easier to keep an eye on them that way, plus he's got his own people in there. The one you refer to as a minister or a priest is his lackey. No one knows where he came from, though probably from somewhere far away, Bohemia or something like that. I wouldn't be surprised if he worked for the sheriff... The sheriff and the mayor do whatever they want... This whole heresy thing is more of a diversion. It's there if they need to use it, although that's not what they're really after. But like I said, I'm completely out of the loop and I like it that way. This is not going to end well."

Blair was intrigued by this explanation which the old man took a long time to get out and which didn't make much sense. "But aren't you this flock's shepherd?" he asked appalled. "How could you let this happen?"

"Ha!" answered the minister dismissively. "I, Sir, am the shepherd of exactly four mangy goats, three hens and a rooster, that is, if he's still alive because I haven't heard him all morning."

"That's because you don't wake up early enough," mumbled Bob. "You must be very lazy."

"At my age, and with this gout that lays me up constantly, not to mention the dead-end track they've put me on, it wouldn't make any difference if I didn't wake up at all!"

"And why do you suppose that there are so many discontented people here?" Blair asked.

"Well people are always discontented," retorted the minister. "You know how it is: last year drought, this year too much rain. The only difference is that this time there are a lot of them, a whole lot... And the sheriff and the mayor hold all the power; I can't do anything. Boston is far away and the Archbishop, who doesn't know much of anything anyway, insists that I stay here..."

"But what about that man with the tattoos?" asked Bob.

"Master Harley?"

"Ah! So it is Marlon. I thought as much. But, then ... I don't understand anything anymore. That means that you too are a part of this masquerade..."

"Marlon who? Dick, Dick Harley is the man you must be referring to—fat, large..."

"His name is Dick?"

"What else would it be? Dick Harley—I'm the one who baptized him."

"In the clearing they were calling him Sire or Sire of all Sires..."

The old man walked up to Blair squinting his eyes maliciously, "Listen, most of my teeth may be gone, and most of my mind too, but you're not going to get me to tell you any more about this. I already told the others everything I know, and God knows plenty have come through here asking. As for those books," he added gesturing towards a niche filled with disheveled old books, "if that's what you came for, know that I have every right to keep them here as the shepherd of this community, as you yourself put it. I can't protect my flock from Satan very well if I don't know all his tricks, can I?"

Blair walked towards the niche, but couldn't see very much in the darkened room. "I don't see why you're so defensive when I haven't meant any harm," he said convinced that the only way to get any useful information from this surly old man was to appeal to his goodwill.

"Yes, I'm defensive! I'm defensive and try to avoid everything. That's why I would like to get away from here as soon as possible. That is, before the hunt starts..."

"Calm down," continued Bob in a softer voice, "I'm not here to interrogate you. Just tell me, how is it that the flock you herd and that, I presume, comes to your church on Sundays and holidays, spends its nights in that clearing..."

"I already told you," the minister cut him off, "it's only a way of keeping everyone under control. That's what both the sheriff and the mayor want. They're actually only keeping an eye on certain people ... certain women ... but things have gotten out of hand and word has spread too far—all the way to London. It's impossible that they wouldn't have heard. We have *witches* here—that is the hunt I'm referring to. You know how it is: when things aren't going well there has to be a scapegoat to take on everyone's sins. I didn't want to be involved—it just so happens that I don't believe in witches."

Blair had a sudden sense of *déjà vu*, as if he had taken part in this conversation once before, but, despite his shockingly good memory, he could not remember when nor how it had ended.

"Amy," he stumbled, "a certain Anne who..."

But he was unable to finish his question because at that exact moment the door opened noisily and four soldiers entered wearing black uniforms with shields hanging off their shoulders and swords in their holsters. The one who appeared to be the leader of the band stopped in front of the minister and looked at him with a certain measure of disgust, "Why don't you answer? We yelled for you several times."

Bob stood up from his precarious stool and confronted him, "He was talking to me. I didn't hear anything either!"

Frowning, the leader turned to Bob, but one of the other soldiers whispered something in his ear and all four bowed deeply. "A thousand apologies, Your Highness," he said bringing forward the medallion that had made walking so difficult and that Blair had hung at his back. "We didn't want to disturb you, but your protection has been entrusted solely to us. Though now we realize that, given the circumstances, the minister would be the first person you would want to talk to."

"Hah! The Lord Protector!" the old man said staring amazedly at the medallion. "I knew that the rumors had made it all the way to London. What can I say: Am I a good one for telling all sorts of stories in front of Your Highness? You will, I don't doubt, forgive the ranting of a run-down country minister..."

"Quite the opposite," said Bob looking at the leader of his supposed personal guard, "everything you have told me is of the utmost interest, and, seeing the confidential nature of our talk and all the answers it could yield, I would like to continue undisturbed at once."

"With all due respect, I must remind Your Grace that it is impossible, at least for the time being. The council meets at ten o'clock, and they are waiting for you."

Bob could feel the chain from which the heavy medallion hung digging into his neck and would have liked to move it again. In the end, he settled for passing it underneath the leather collar of the large vest he was wearing. That felt much less oppressive.

"In that case, let's go!" he said, and the guards, clicking their heels once, stood back to allow him to exit the cottage. He stopped suddenly. "Ah! I've forgotten something important. Wait here, I'll be right back."

He opened the door without warning and caught the minister taking several books out of the niche as if he intended to hide them. "Do you read Arabic?" he asked.

"Yes. And Aramaic. We all protect ourselves however we know best," answered the minister caught in the act. "Please forgive me Lord Ian Blair."

Actually, Bob wanted to ask him about Amy, Anne,

Amaradaminda, or whatever her name was—that girl who seemed to be the sister he had always and at the same time never known and whom he had found and lost all on the same day. But the name that the minister called him stopped all his interest in further conversation. He felt the room spin, and saw the old man bring him water in the same filthy cup he had offered earlier. Blair drank, wiped his thick beard with his hand, opened the door and walked out into the harsh morning light.

Present Day New York

Walking into his office on the second floor of the Supreme Court building, Judge Robert Blair immediately noticed a change about which he had thought for a long time. However, at this moment, the change did not give him any pleasure. The papers, mail, and files that usually covered his desk, the shelves, and even the two extra chairs were now completely organized, marked with typed labels and arranged in several neat piles on a book shelf he almost did not recognize. He pressed the intercom button a few times and the clerk on call came right away.

"Norman, what is going on here?" asked Bob.

"Good morning, Sir," replied Norman. "I hope you're feel-ing better..."

"I asked you what's going on here. What are all these

things?"

The clerk threw a confused look around the room and said, "Oh, you mean how clean it is. Isn't it incredible? Yesterday, when we got the message that you weren't feeling well and would not be coming in, the new secretary started working right away. Sir, I'm telling you, she's very skilled. She worked for almost ten hours, but I've never seen anything like it in all my life—she organized everything, she got the supply guys in gear, got some new folders and printed labels, she even managed to write a few memos on the computer that we all thought was broken. There's a special folder on your desk with documents for you to sign, and all the papers she didn't know what to do with are in the top drawer. I supervised the whole thing, and I can tell you that I'm impressed by her efficiency. Very good choice, Sir, if you don't mind me saying!"

Blair sank slowly into his armchair. "This new secretary, Norman, was she hired by Human Resources? I don't remember any applicants responding to the ad I placed last month..."

"Oh Sir, it's clear you really haven't been feeling well. It's no wonder too; there's been a nasty flu going around this fall. You sent her here yourself with a handwritten recommendation. I made a copy before I sent her to Human Resources. Do you want to see it?"

Bob feared that showing too much distrust would do nothing but cause his subordinate to become, quite rightly, suspicious. Coupled with the compassion Norman had expressed earlier, this annoyed Blair more and more. "No, there's no need, Norman. Thank you. We're talking about Amy, right? Amy..."

"Amy Baxter, Sir. This Miss Baxter will undoubtedly make our lives here much easier. Assuming she keeps it up. You know what they say: all good things…"

Blair was bothered by the familiar and somewhat patronizing tone this underling was taking and resolved that he would not hesitate to fire him at the earliest opportunity.

"Alright, send Miss Baxter to me as soon as she arrives."

"She's been here since seven o'clock, but they called her down to Human Resources to fill out her paperwork."

"Alright."

Upon Norman's departure, Blair closed his eyes and rested his head in his hands. All he remembered was the party at Harley's, those idiotic taunts about *caveat emptor*, the girl who had sat on his knee and the feeling that he was holding the sister he had never had. Everything else was extremely foggy, but it began coming back to him in odd fragments.

He had woken up at home the next morning. He must have called the Court. Then he dozed all day without getting out of bed. Carol wasn't home … The walk through the forest, the conversation with an old, stubborn country minister, some strange liturgy … Something about witches in Englewood, Massachusetts, centuries ago … then his own name, Blair, and himself being referred to as Lord Protector … the minister's belief that a witch hunt was imminent…

Amy walked in without knocking. "Norman tells me you're feeling better! Thank you very much; I'm sure you put in a good word for my salary. I'm almost embarrassed. It's a fortune!"

There were butterflies in Bob's stomach and he felt suddenly feverish as he had when, as a child, he was ill with measles.

"Amy, I should be thanking you! This office has never looked like this. As for Norman, I think you've won him over completely. Maybe it will inspire him to do some work himself—God knows I haven't managed this in two years!"

"Don't say that!" Amy replied, her whole being exuding a naturalness that Bob would never tire of admiring. "It's true he's a little slow, but he has a lot to learn. All he wants to do is be a judge."

"I know," answered Bob with a bored air, "but let's move on. I must apologize if at Marlon's, I mean in Harley's house, I behaved perhaps too familiarly, or ... I had had too much to drink, presumably like everyone else."

Amy looked at him for a long time with the same gaze that had made him leave the clearing in Englewood.

"But you didn't drink at all!" exclaimed Amy. "You talked to me almost the entire time. No one's ever been so nice to me! You know ... you told me all about Carol too. I think you had a fever; it's this nasty twenty-four hour virus; they were talking about it on the news."

"Oh, now I'm embarrassed," said Blair in a dead tone. "Perhaps I wasn't at my best..."

"In that case," Amy interrupted him, "I'm happy it worked out this way because you offered me the job recommendation without asking me anything about who I am or what I can do. Isn't it extraordinary?"

"Yes, everything's been extraordinary lately," mumbled Bob lost in thought. "Not to even mention the way you've organized everything here. I should consider myself very lucky!"

"Don't mention it," she said shaking her head and revealing the sapphire crucifix. "There's an explanation for everything. I worked part-time for a few years in the law library at New York University. That's where I met Mr. Harley."

"Marlon reads?!" Bob exclaimed in perfectly reasonable shock.

He could not take his eyes off the sapphire cross, the same he had seen dangling from the neck of the girl in the clearing at Englewood. He had to admit that she was not Amy despite the astonishing resemblance. "Amy," he asked, "where did you get that crucifix?"

"It's sapphire," the girl replied, "and it's the only valuable object I own. My grandmother gave it to me. She got it from her grandmother, but no one in the family wore it until me because the chain it hangs on was broken. See?" she added and pulled the collar of her shirt aside with true grace, to reveal a chain that was half gold and half silver or some similar metal.

"I couldn't afford gold ... Someday, maybe ... Regardless, I wouldn't give this cross up for anything in the world. You won't believe this, but it makes me feel like myself. I think I was a much more complicated and difficult person before I started wearing it ... But why am I carrying on like this? You should stop me. One of my biggest faults is that sometimes I talk too much. We have two cases coming up next month—one of them has to do with the Basset property in Katonah..."

"Oh no, please! Not again! I hope it's nothing to do with ghosts again," Blair muttered under his breath, though, at this point, he had little interest in anything that would be happening the next day, let alone next week or next month.

"I have no idea yet, but they're going to send me the brief sometime today. Now, if you don't mind, I'm going to get back to work. We just got some letters."

Bob had to tell himself that it would be completely inappropriate to stop her, though he felt the urge to talk to her, to know that she was always nearby. When Amy opened the door to leave, Bob felt the butterflies flutter in his stomach again and experienced an acute pain of separation.

Norman, who had presumably knocked several times before opening the door, found him prone, staring fixedly at the ceiling and looking pale and sickly. "Can I bring you an Alka-Seltzer, Sir? Or maybe some warm tea?" he asked. "Perhaps you shouldn't have come in today. The barometer is falling..."

Blair resented the protective tone this petty idiot had adopted. "No, thank you, Norman. It's just one of those days, you know ... Anyway, what have we here?"

"The Prosecution's memorandum from last week, two requests for postponement, along with all the necessary paperwork which I have personally reviewed, Ms. Baxter's employment papers, and three news clippings discussing the decision in *Collins vs. Benson*—I thought they might interest you," jabbered Norman very pleased with himself.

"Fine, very well!" answered Bob with a heavy tone, and

Norman quickly left the office.

Bob was trying to remember who else had offered him warm tea recently ... The minister! The minister from Englewood in that filthy little room. Now he remembered what he had been meaning to do ever since he had woken up that morning: go to the library. He'd sign the papers, but to hell with the clippings and Norman's servility.

When he reached Amy's employment papers he froze. On the top line he could clearly read: *Baxter, Amaradaminda*. He tried hard to remain calm, as calm as possible, then pressed the second button on his phone. Amy walked in carrying her notepad.

"You won't need that ... Amy, tell me please," babbled Bob despite his resolve to remain perfectly calm, "what's with this name here? Come, look..."

The girl picked up on his agitated state and her discomfort was obvious as she approached the desk. "Oh!" she sighed with relief. "It's my real name—a strange family tradition. It's caused me nothing but trouble with the mail, in college, at the bank, everywhere. My mother, grandmother and great grandmother all had the same name. I don't even know how many generations back. It's ridiculous; that's why everyone calls me Amy. Only my colleagues at the library liked to call me Amaradaminda."

"Of course!" said Blair signing the paper. "At the library. Everything is perfectly clear. Thank you! Please give all these things back to Norman, and please be kind enough to throw the three clippings in the garbage."

The Law Library at New York University is only ten minutes away from the Supreme Court, and Bob decided to walk there hoping that it would give him a chance to make some sense of his jumbled thoughts and gain some perspective on his own involvement in this story. Crossing Bleeker Street toward Washington Square, however, he realized that this was a lost cause, otherwise why would he have left his office in the middle of the day like this?

He knew the associate director of the library well, so he had no trouble immediately obtaining a complete bibliography dealing with the Massachusetts witch trials. Almost all the books on the list were available except for two that dealt with the physical trials that the witches were subjected to, and that had been borrowed by Harley's firm for two months. Bob decided not to jump to any hasty conclusions, but nonetheless could not help thinking that nothing seemed to be coincidental anymore. He would have to come to some conclusions eventually, if not right away.

Speed reading through a few of the books about the witches of Salem served only to strengthen his opinion that people write more and more superficially and frivolously about legal history. He pored a bit more closely over one volume that offered a succinct chronology of all the events of the trials not just in Salem, but in the entire region at the end of the seventeenth century. He had almost given up when the name *Anne*

Predator aka *Amaradaminda* next to the date September 22, 1692, caught his eye. He searched feverishly through the index, then through the pages that referred to the trial. She had been sentenced to hang for the crime of incantation, defined by the Court according to the norms established in London by Lord Judge Coke as the act of someone *qui carminibus aut cantiunculis Daemonem adjurat.*

"The minister, that bastard!" muttered Blair indignantly under his breath. "He fed me that tale about the heretical liturgy being just some sort of distraction." Otherwise the rest of the record of Lord Protector Ian Blair's interrogations was rather boring. The proceedings were a true insult to the art of jurisprudence in that any missing evidence was made up and accepted tacitly in most cases.

As for Amaradaminda, Ms. Baxter, the library's employees remembered her well. She had worked there and was a lovely person, as his friend, the associate director, was to confirm. She had left the position a few weeks earlier for a new job in a law firm.

Arriving home, Bob felt exhausted. He had to admit that the flu was affecting him more than he would have liked; he drank a hot grog took a sleeping pill and went to bed without checking the messages on his answering machine.

Blair heard a litany of voices and felt the sharp smell of smoke in his nostrils. Sneaking through the trees he discovered that the clearing was full of soldiers. In the center of the clearing the remnants of the barrel altar and of numerous clothes were still smoldering. He turned around and carefully made his way back to the village.

"You're late," the minister greeted him with a grimace from his muddy yard. "But I see that you haven't wasted any time unleashing these hunters and you have made me, in a way, your accomplice against my will. Lord Ian Blair, this is the last thing I need here!"

"I'm not ... I'm not who you think I am ... I must admit this despite all evidence to the contrary. But you, you're a liar. You told me that the mass in the clearing was just an act. But now I see that Amy, I mean Anne ... Anne Predator was hanged for *incantatio Daemonem*"

"You must be out of your mind, Lord Blair. Anne Predator (aka Amaradaminda, after all I'm the one who baptized her) was not hanged; though I suppose she could be, maybe even for the reason you mention. There's no reason why they shouldn't start condemning people for heresy. Master Harley turned everyone in; the sheriff and the mayor have spent a fortune. For now she is under arrest like everyone else ... but hanged for *incantatio*? Wherever did you get that idea? Or maybe you're trying to trick me again," finished the old man in disbelief.

"What's today's date?" asked Bob quickly.

"The fifteenth," answered the minister. "September fifteenth."

"Good! We still have a week. Because, believe me, she will be hanged on September 22. Don't ask me how I know. You would think it beyond nature. Now I have to go, but I will be back, and I may need your help."

"You know those books you caught me hiding earlier? This is exactly what they deal with. Nothing is beyond nature. Nature is the essence of all that exists and cannot be what it is not, so nothing can be beyond it. I for one am perfectly at peace with this. You, however, don't seem to be at peace with anything, not with the hunt, nor with the executions. You always find yourself where you shouldn't be, and you're terrified that you'll be too late by the time you get to where you're going. Why did you ever become a judge? Give me just one reason, in a simple sentence without provisos or rationalizations!"

This last sentence the old man declared in a tone so completely antithetical to his appearance in this pathetic yard that it reminded Bob of the only time he had ever answered that question with just such a shockingly simple sentence. Standing in the deans' room at Harvard Law School he had said, *"I have to!"* Though, obviously, at that time he could not have suspected any of this.

"Professor Hastings!" was all he could utter. "My dear Professor Hastings..."

But all the dignity that the minister had exhibited a moment earlier seemed to have melted, and he was the same poor country minister, dirty and toothless.

"I can't understand what you're saying. I can barely hear. You could very well just be crazy. But regardless, if you do return I'll help you, at least to the extent that someone like me can." With this he stuck his hand in the pot he was carrying and that presumably contained a mixture of water and corn flour that quickly attracted the three hungry hens.

Leaving the yard, Blair was perturbed, but determined not to waste his time trying to uncover any more. Walking towards the Communal Council, it occurred to him that certain questions and answers could, after all, float around independent of those who had originally uttered them. They could show up at any time and place, as if traveling through parallel tunnels until they break out linking independent realities without any logic and creating, maybe for the first time, some sort of *sense*.

"I want to see the evidence relating to the cases of ... let's see ... Hannah Words, Beatrix Summer, Mary Parker, and ... Anne ... Anne Predator," he demanded pretending to be looking over the few sheets of paper that the clerk had placed in front of him.

"Lord Blair," the mayor quickly jumped in, "the evidence dispels any doubt. Master Harley, who is here now awaiting Your Highness's goodwill, has informed us in the utmost detail of everything related to these cases. You know, we retained him so that we would not stir up any suspicions in the community. His extremely precious service could lead to the arrest of the whole lot, as the sheriff can confirm..."

"Ah! Master Harley! Very well! I understand he is a person on whom we can rely totally."

"Of course," piped up the sheriff in an obsequious tone. "He executed all his orders even beyond the call of duty."

"Beyond the call of duty means very zealously. This should be repaid in kind," continued Blair. "Let him be taken to the village square and given fifty lashes across the back. I understand that we will need him again in the future, so the community must not have any doubts about him."

"Pity, Your Highness!" Harley rushed forward ready even to kiss his dirty boots. "Everything I've done has been only out of love for good law. Why should I be punished?"

"This is not punishment, Master Harley," answered Bob, "just a small sacrifice with which we repay the excessively zealous defense of good law. We all want to see it triumph, but good law, by its very nature, triumphs on its own. Everything that goes beyond this, beyond the call of duty as has already been mentioned, is a deviation from nature." Assuring himself that no one else would hear them, he muttered under his breath, "This is what our dear Professor Hastings would have said, isn't it, Marlon? When we meet again, you'll thank me for this."

Moaning, Harley let his entire weight drop into the arms of the guard who took him outside in order to administer the punishment that Blair had just dealt.

A great and long buzz arose from the dignitaries and officials in the room following the incident. Lord Blair, however, seemed to have the whole situation under control. In the end, only the mayor dared to approach Bob hoping to intervene on Harley's behalf. "Your Highness has judged very well, if I may say so; it's just that we have received word from London that the governor, Sir Bradley, should arrive here any day with a new charter written specifically for our colony, Massachusetts, which would remove the need for any proof in cases where the accusation was well founded. Perhaps it would be best if we delayed slightly any discussion of evidence and especially the sentencing of Master Harley to this tribulation that is as clever a political act as it is painful..."

"We'll see. We'll see," answered Blair without hesitation. "London is already quite annoyed with the weaknesses of the administration here. Until then let us continue looking over the evidence so that people won't lose faith in the judicial system."

And so he began hearing an entire series of arguments and depositions, some more some less boring, taking notes as he would have had in his office in Manhattan and collecting evidence for each of the cases, but especially for the one concerning Anne Predator, aka Amaradaminda. With all this jumping around from one date to another, the only thing he considered fortunate was that the blasted charter from London had not arrived yet and that Harley was, at least for now, out of the way and therefore unable to testify in any of the cases.

Regarding Amaradaminda's case, he noted that she had been caught in the rye field near Brewster holding a bunch of the plant which the sheriff brought and laid a few sprigs on Blair's bench. A subsequent search of her home revealed three full bags of this kind of rye. For the notary from Streamsea, the only legal authority in the room, everything was very clear. The girl had tainted the field earlier with satanic incantations and had been caught while checking on the results of her work. No wonder the rye crops had been so bad that year! Blair objected that he saw no possible reason why the girl would have three bags of the dried plant at home, especially if it really was satanic, but the notary insisted that Satan always had his own ways, which often contradicted all rationalism, precisely to trick vigilant judges. Everyone in the room appeared to agree with him, and the mayor went so far as to utter "Amen" and hurried to remove the offensive plants from Blair's bench. Bob, however, managed to make one sprig disappear, sliding it carefully underneath his roomy vest.

Once matters turned to questions of procedure, the discussion became more animated. The notary insisted that it would be best for all suspects to be tried the same day and that the various tests that served to prove one's status as a witch should be administered as quickly as possible so that eventually all could be hanged at the same time. This would have an excellent effect on the community, putting the holy fear in all who needed it and discouraging anyone from rebelling or asking unnecessary questions. Blair, using the local administration's own weapons, maintained that such a block treatment would not be appropriate given the fact that the new charter from London would, as the mayor had said, arrive any moment repealing the need for evidence and opening, then and only then, the legal way for a mass trial and execution of all the suspects. Until the charter's arrival, however, even the notary must admit that the only legal course of action was to try each case individually and check all the evidence.

The mayor, who had been dozing off for the last half hour of the proceedings, was so flattered to hear Lord Blair mention his name that he approved the idea immediately.

"But Lord Blair," insisted the notary, "I hope that you will agree to begin administering the trials to everyone regardless of the evidence. The Privy Council itself advises that once proof is obtained using infallible methods all doubts cease."

"Hmm, that depends," said Blair trying to remember what the trials consisted of. "What are you thinking of?"

"I was thinking," the notary from Streamsea answered quickly, eager to demonstrate his competence in these matters, "that, since we have already had six executions, it would be best to skip the physical examination for the Devil's marks, as well as the trial by water, both of which are considered mild and ineffective even by Lord Keeper Guildford, and move directly to the trial by blood and the trial by fire which are not only extremely efficient but, through the suffering they entail, often lead to immediate confessions of guilt as well as spectacular conversions!"

Blair truly hated this petty functionary and his fanaticism though both the mayor and the sheriff appeared to trust him absolutely. He had managed to horrify everyone in the room.

"I'm afraid I must contradict you there," answered Blair in a determined tone. "Not too long ago, in Leicester, a court declared these two trials 'bad law' because they insist on Satan's powers instead of glorifying the Lord." He was very convincing. The result came soon as he heard some people comment that, yes, what could be more appropriate than that the law glorify God. "Therefore, we will start with the basic trials, those that the law recommends clearly and specifically: the physical examination, the marks of the Devil..."

No sooner had Blair spoken these words than the door flew open and the head of his guard burst into the room, "Lord Blair, your Highness, the church is on fire!"

The minister was standing in the yard holding a bucket of water and watching the smoke rise out of the church as it burned steadily. Hundreds of people had already gathered there carrying pitchforks, ladders and axes.

"Gather everyone in the square," he said sharply to the mayor. "Tell them that a handful of coals from the minister's chimney, which evidently hasn't been cleaned in a while, fell onto the roof of the church. It's clear that that's where the fire started. The sheriff should maintain the best possible order among the population. I don't want to hear any rumors about witchcraft; this would undermine the importance of the impending trials just when we are trying so hard to distinguish the cowardly work of Satan from things that are unimportant and coincidental."

The mayor stared at Blair incredulously and swallowed hard. "Very well, Lord Blair, if you say so. But the sheriff thought this would be a great opportunity to tie everything together: the heretic masses, the poor harvest, the spells that the suspects are ready to reveal through the trial by blood, and now, the burning of the church."

"You must not be getting enough sleep," answered Bob finally understanding everything. "What you are saying makes no sense. How could the sheriff have known that this would happen? Or maybe now you think that he too is possessed?"

"God forbid!" exclaimed the mayor realizing that he had tipped his hand. "Your Grace is right. I must be very tired. Everything will be done as you ordered."

Blair dismissed the guard and, leaving word that they should not be disturbed, entered the minister's hovel. "Who was it?" he asked the minister as soon as he was inside.

"Master Harley and his men," answered the latter lost in thought. "Dick's brow was deeply furrowed, and he could barely move. I saw him well."

"I took care of him," said Blair. "So these bastards are following through with their plan, point by point, while they wait for the new charter to arrive from London. We must hurry! Do you by any chance know what this is, other than plain rye?" he asked pulling the plant out of his vest.

The old man looked it over for a long time, and then walked to the little dirty window which afforded just a sliver of light. "Hmm, look at that! It's rye alright, but there's something else: *Claviceps purpurea*; it's a fungus, a parasite. They also call it *ergot*. Where did you find it?"

"Amy ... I mean Anne Predator was caught holding it in the rye field near Brewster. Apparently they found another three bags of it at her house."

The minister fell heavily onto his bed. "But it's perfectly

clear. Without even knowing it the girl was weeding the rye field! You can make a tea with sedative properties from rye tainted with *claviceps purpurea*. Any healer knows that."

"Are you sure?" asked Bob taking notes again.

Instead of answering, the old man searched through a sack that was hanging above the niche with the books and pulled out several dried plants identical to the one Blair had brought. "The fields near Brewster?" he continued, "Do you mean the ones near the water?! That's it: the rye grew there better than anywhere else this year. Now we know why!"

ANOTHER ASIDE

Bob sensed that he had slept unusually well, perhaps because of his illness (he always slept well when he had a fever), perhaps also because of the strong grog. He woke full of energy and his first thought was to go see John Winkler, his former Harvard classmate, who had been the center of some extremely animated controversies about ten years earlier but was now forgotten by almost everyone.

Johnny Winkler had been a paradoxical type even as an undergrad when he had taken to publishing, under various pseudonyms, the craziest articles in otherwise serious magazines and newspapers. He had made a bit of a name for himself with the joke he played on *The Boston Journal and Digest* and *The Christian Independent Monitor* in which he published, under different names, articles sustaining opposing points of view in a very delicate and scholarly debate on the gender of angels. He was accepted to Harvard Law School in the wake of this "glory." But he had not been an impressive student; he cared very little, if at all, about grades and even less about what his professors or classmates thought of him. He spent all his time reading, and his close friends could attest that he never slept more than four hours a night, usually directly on the floor as his bed was covered in books.

Bob had always seen him as some kind of somber savant. Knowing about Johnny's esoteric reading only confused him further, and made him keep his distance somewhat. The scandal hit two years after graduation. John Winkler, an Assistant Professor of Law at some little known school on the West Coast, published two massive volumes on cases involving paranormal phenomena in Europe and the United States—witches, shamans, mediums, psychics, hypnotists ... The information was augmented by Winkler's personal commentary, in which he distinguished between *true* witches and *false* witches and between just and unjust sentences. TV, radio, every newspaper, magazine and professional journal, even the sordid tabloids had printed excerpts from the book, interviews with the author, and columns dealing with the subject.

Winkler lost his job at the university in the wake of the controversy. He responded with a nonchalance bordering on irresponsibility in the ultra calculated world of lawmakers. Robert Blair had written a column in *The New York Law Journal* that was as favorable to the work (he praised without reservation the minute documentation, the superior style, but carefully avoided its more disturbing elements) as it was ultimately useless. Johnny Winkler, however, had been so profoundly flattered by Blair's gesture that he had shown up one night on the latter's doorstep, drunk and agitated, but ready to extend his hand in friendship. It was in their apartment (at this time Carol was still, in some ways, a part of his life) that Johnny had suffered a terrible attack of shivering and had lost consciousness. Bob called an ambulance and took care of all the details until his friend was ultimately diagnosed with epilepsy (John subsequently admitted that he had suffered from such attacks ever since he was a child). He then secured some hefty benefits for Winkler from the wealthy Alumni Association of Harvard and later, without Winkler's knowledge, collected a series of donations which allowed the former to be admitted to a sanatorium at Amerhurst in upstate New York, a veritable paradise from which Johnny had sent the following short but meaningful letter:

My dear and excellent friend Bob,

That which you can see often does not exist. That which cannot be seen sometimes is the only truth and brings all other things into being. I am happy for both of us that things have worked out as they have. As I do not believe in coincidences—in fact I wrote as much in that damned book!—I will not thank you now, as I should. Everything is just a fragment, forever waiting for the next part.

May you be blessed!

Yours, from another world,

John Winkler

Walking into the charming garden of the sanatorium, tired after a four-hour drive, Bob realized that Winkler had been right to sign his letter "from another world." Everything here was so calm and calming, in the gentle sun of an Indian summer, with the main building, a gigantic Victorian house, silhouetted like a castle against the blue sky. His fatigue left him immediately. But it was not easy to get in to see John Winkler as he had an unusually large number of visitors. Blair insisted on waiting until all the other guests had left, although two more people appeared while he was waiting and he allowed them to go in ahead of him.

"Bob!" Johnny exclaimed when he saw Bob's figure hesitate in the doorway and look around amazed. "Bob! What a surprise! What I mean is what a surprise today, now! I have to confess that I have been waiting for you for a long time, but even I didn't know when you would come."

Blair let these words slide past him as he surveyed the large, bright room with its shelves full of books on every wall and a large wooden desk piled high with files and law books. "My God, John, everything here looks better than my own office at the Court in Manhattan! What's going on?"

"Oh you mean this," replied a relaxed Winkler pointing at his surroundings. "It is how I repay my small debt to society. I help however I can, and God knows there are plenty of people in a bind."

"Johnny," continued Bob, "you don't mean that all those

people who made me wait for two hours..."

"Yes! They're *cases*, real *cases*. This was my great weakness. For years I got lost in hypothetical thinking, all so sterile and artificial. And perhaps I was punished for that. Here I discovered the bold litigant part of myself, *pro bono*, of course. I wouldn't take anyone's money; in fact sometimes I even pay for some of my poorer clients' cab fares home. In the last few years I have won a total of forty-two cases," he said looking quickly through a notebook maintained in the most meticulous handwriting, "for a grand total of (and we're speaking of virtual sums here) one million two hundred thirty thousand dollars!"

"But Johnny, this is malpractice! You should be careful."

"Relax Bob! My dear law-abiding Bob! Malpractice refers only to the real world. From a nuthouse you can do almost anything you want, within certain limits, of course. I wouldn't be surprised if this was the only place where a true lawyer could honestly say: *The law has to be moral first, or it is no law at all.*"

Blair was even more surprised when Winkler, exceedingly proud of himself, enumerated in detail several cases that had been won (even at the Supreme Court of New York) by individuals who had shown up, for one reason or another, without legal representation. There was no doubt; with his great memory Bob immediately recognized the names of the litigants in question.

It took Robert Blair almost four hours to fully explain the reasons that had brought him there. While Bob spoke, Winkler moved constantly, mumbling sentence fragments, exclaiming, gathering books from the shelves that lined the room, taking quick notes. Bob gave him all the details as best he could, starting with the growing number of cases dealing with *karmic* properties, the evening at Marlon Harley's and everything else that had led him to 1692 Englewood.

"Bob," said Winkler at the end of the confession, "I really don't know if you're ready for this. What I am about to tell you may make you doubt me and our friendship..."

"John," answered Bob exhausted by the whole unsettling afternoon, "the reason I came to you is that you are my last resort. You're the only one who not only knew, but wrote down in black and white, the things that I am more and more convinced I am experiencing and cannot make sense of."

Instead of answering, Winkler opened a book that displayed on two colorful pages Lord Ian Blair's family tree. It started with King Richard the Lion Hearted and ended in 1799 with a certain Master William Blair, a notary in New England ... "Yes," said Bob calmly. "He married Martha McNeill and had three children. The boy, Peter Blair was a judge in Boston and is my great grandfather—I just found it out a few days ago from a book. But it's more than that. I'm suffering from a sense of guilt, perhaps even stronger than appropriate, and this all happened over the past few weeks. What bothers me a lot more though is this sister that I feel like I can no longer live without, this Amy or whatever you want to call her based on everything I've told you. I also have the feeling that everything that was happening there and then concerns my inner being, or at least that's how it seems to me."

"Bob," said Winkler gravely, "you have walked into a Gnostic scenario without being in any way prepared (except perhaps by your natural aversion to anything 'impure') and you've begun to discover the basis of alchemy through unmediated experience. Maybe this whole process, starting with the *karmic* property cases, which you yourself said seemed to be seeking you out, was set in motion by your own feelings of guilt. These things are so difficult to explain in words though, and everything that I can deduce from your stories leads towards a single conclusion: a word that covers two irreconcilable opposites, but which I am afraid to say!"

"Why me, Johnny? Why should all this happen to me?"

"Oh, Bob! The way in which you phrase that question won't lead us too far. This is an egg and chicken situation. Maybe you yourself provoked all this in exactly the way in which you are seeing it and in which you feel so implicated."

Blair took up a tense pacing of the room. It was clear that he did not understand much of what was happening.

"Part of your consciousness, of which you had never been aware," continued Winkler, "came into contact with the *fundamental eon* that transcends all space and time, disappears in one place only to appear again who knows when and where. It is the latency that keeps the world from vanishing. Without conceding this, everything that has been happening to you is nothing but a dizzying cocktail of elements thrown together, presumably, by your own sensitivity. For example, you maintain that you witnessed that strange alchemic mass in the clearing in Englewood. In the same way, you took the interrogator's questions and the connection between Jesus and Adam and wove them into a story that includes Marlon. Something purely intuitive, probably influenced by the conversation that had taken place that evening. I had nicknamed Marlon, "Sire" as far back as college, though you would have had no way of knowing that. I could prove to you that the religious service did not take place there, but in a completely different place and time. It's a well known mass dedicated to the Hungarian king Ladislav by a Melchior Cibinensis, a well-educated Romanian utopian based in Sibiu. Alas, the poor man was executed in Prague in 1531. All these things, old man, happen independently of us in spaces and times that run parallel to each other and only occasionally superimpose on each other, locking into a sort of *nodal point*, if you understand what I'm trying to say. And when these nodal points intersect they inflame the consciousness and all of a sudden we wake up as some sort of *identity*. It's entirely possible that you are one of these. You are some sort of *transistor*, God help me, for a continuum that only rarely makes itself known. Not to even mention that evoking Hermes Trismegistus isn't even a part of Melchior's liturgy, but is a fundamental component of the so called *Corpus Hermeticum*, a collection of Greek texts from the second and third centuries BC. The fact that you have integrated it here is due only to your obsession with rebirth! That's exactly why, from the beginning in Harley's dining room, where you probably remained the entire time, you felt, as you yourself have admitted, dead."

John opened a book and Bob read: *Addam et processum sub*

forma missae, a Nicolao Cibinesi Transilvano, ad Ladislaum Ungariae et Bohemiae regem olim missum[11] followed by the words that the minister had said in the clearing and which, at the time, he could only partially understand, and the beautiful hymn *Ave, Praeclara Maris Stella* after the Gospel according to Luke.

"This is it!" exclaimed Blair. "And then the Virgin appeared as the embodiment of Botticeli's *Spring*. Tell me, what sect uses this service?"

Johnny Winkler lowered his head into his hands, then stood up and sat back down several times. "Bob, these are very serious things, things for which it is worth losing your mind. Perhaps you are not quite ready ... A young scientist in Chicago who had been studying the Gnostic and alchemic implications of Botticelli's *Spring* was recently shot dead. As for the fact that you were not there to see the Transubstantiation it's no big surprise. It was your own transformation that was taking place and that continues even now!"

Blair furrowed his brow and searched for an answer. "Yes, Johnny, you're probably right, in a way that, to be perfectly honest, is inaccessible to me. Though I do not think you are in the least crazy, I do believe that you have reached your conclusion exactly because you have studied these matters for so long. Whereas I am the epitome of rational thought, of the success of cogitation over all that is illogical, and am now experiencing exactly those insufferable things that you know so

---

[11] I will add the act sent as a missive some time ago by Nicolaus of Cibinium, the Transylvanian, to Ladislau, the King of Hungary and Bohemia.

well. I do not want to be initiated, because I am much more concerned with action. I have to *do that which is my duty to do* as the Gospel according to Luke says."

"In that case," Winkler rushed in excitedly, "you should know that you really are dead, or at least you should be if, as you say, you can no longer live and are ready to relinquish your flesh and bone existence and just *be*! Ultimately, this is why you heard what you heard, namely the secret of the Great Art: *Fundamentum vero artis est corporum solutio!*

"Yes, yes, that is exactly what I heard!" confirmed Bob, frightening Winkler with his innocence.

"But, my dear Bob, your alchemic transgression, in other words your pure rebirth, cannot happen without the help of your *soror mystica*, who, unfortunately for you, has been dead since September 22, 1692, when she was hanged."

"That's not entirely true," Blair opposed him. "Amy is alive, and wears Amaradaminda's sapphire cross around her neck. Her words were meant only for me. Now that I have spoken to you I understand those strange words so much better: *"If I were to be descending / I might take away your strife / And your knowledge of true longing!"*

"Of course," said Winkler looking through some books, "Anne Predator's sapphire, which this great granddaughter, Amy, has decided to wear, is the symbol of chastity, piety, and fidelity. It's clear here in this book, *in some traditions, lapis is called the 'sapphire flower'*. That is precisely why you were able to meet Amy, your mystic sister, the only one who could help you transcend and be born pure as you long to, though you yourself cannot say why. But Bob, think about the consequences. She cannot exist unless you cause her to be born. And in order for her to be born you would have to overturn the sentence in the case of Anne Predator, *aka* Amaradaminda."

"John Barney Winkler, you finally understand! Is this not the reason why I allowed myself to be identified as my ancestor, Lord Ian Blair? Maybe I don't need too much esoteric knowledge concerning the Gnostic/alchemic experiences I had there. Maybe some people, my old friend, jump directly to action while being perfectly ignorant of the subtext, while others pay for the sins of their sterile research in sanatoriums like you, in drink like McCormick, or in intellectual vanity like my dear Brad Wilkins. With him I have nonetheless shared some of what has been happening to me. All I want to do is to re-try that case, and perhaps all those that fell under Blair's jurisdiction."

"Bob, Bob! Things are once again more complicated than you think."

"I want you to tell me about the marks of the Devil, the first test recommended by the Privy Council, because I have decided that is how we will start. All the others seemed unbearably atrocious."

"Let's see," said Winkler warming up to the game. "You would have to judge according to the law in effect in England established by Archbishop Judge Norman Welsey, because it is before 1703. Yes, the body of the suspect will be searched by midwives for anything that is missing or that shouldn't be there."

"Amy!" exclaimed Bob, "Amy is missing a rib. That's how she was born; I remember she told me that night at Marlon's. I will have to avoid this test. But how?"

"Not necessarily," answered Johnny reading. "If the mid-wife who assisted at her birth testifies that she was born so, there is no problem."

"Hmm. I could arrange that with the minister's help. I trust him."

"It's just that, as you can see from the record of the trials, they only ever used four midwives and they were all in league with the mayor and the sheriff. You would know that if you had read my book carefully."

"I can take that chance," answered Blair after thinking for a time. "What's with that 'trial by blood'?"

"That one you should avoid at any cost. The administra-tion has people whom they paid to have hysterical fits, unbear-able pains, and loss of consciousness just from seeing the blood of a suspected witch!"

"Aha!" said Blair taking notes. "Then this trial will be excluded. As for walking on coals, I will not use it under any circumstances. Regarding the ergot or rye's death as it's also called, that certain *claviceps purpurea* I have no problems. The old man told me everything, and I think he will show up in court to defend Anne."

"That's possible," answered Winkler. "Let's see. History tells us that the minister of Englewood would have died ten months later, and, perhaps in this regard, nothing has to change. Whether or not he is our dear Professor Hastings, as you suspect, who knows and ultimately what does it matter when we are dealing with all these parallel tunnels? The only important things are the ones you yourself identify. But look how strange: here in this old book of apocryphal accounts, it says that Anne Predator *aka* Amaradaminda spent the night before her execution singing in her cell. *I won't have a tomb or stone in the cemetery. Nor will children ever be born of me.*"

"So me neither," said Bob smiling sadly.

"You aren't her child, Bob. She is your mystic sister and will only be helping you to be reborn. That is if everything works according to your plan."

"It will work, Johnny. It will work. That is why I will go back there."

"Good luck," said Winkler. "I must confess that I, even with all my knowledge, am powerless in the face of your determination. I'm sorry that I can't help you with anything. But then again, that is exactly as it should be. You have to be born naked and completely defenseless, and you must draw your strength from this supreme weakness."

"I came to you for advice, John. That is more helpful to me than anything else."

"Good bye then, my friend," added Winkler. "As for the charter from London, which you seem to have completely forgotten, and that could mess up all your plans, don't worry. It won't arrive in time; I have an old score to settle with Governor Bradley..."

The two men shook hands warmly by the large gate at the entrance of the now darkened park.

Blair drove straight home through thick, diagonal rain. He thought to himself that it would be best if he stopped at a hotel on the way, but he was not in the least tired and, in fact, he did not relax until at last he threw himself on his bed, exhausted and wet.

Stepping out of the car, he felt the viscous mud under his soles. He passed his hand through his thick beard murmuring, "Yes, you will have a tomb in the cemetery, and your children will mourn you!"

The rain had stopped. It was cool, almost cold, and the night seemed to be young. He wandered before finding the road to the village because the moon was barely showing its face through the clouds. He felt his way into the burnt church's yard, walked around piles of rubble and burnt wood, and only then realized that there was a light on in the minister's room. He opened the door all the way without bothering to knock.

He heard someone say: "Blair, bless you!" and couldn't help thinking of Professor Hastings' gentle exhortations. "Blair, Blair, you're late again!"

"I went to see Johnny," said Blair trying to trip him up. "I'm sorry. You'll be dead in ten months. I hope this won't prevent you from helping me."

The old man stood up, and, if he were surprised, he skillfully hid any emotion.

"We all die in one way or another, sooner or later, and only the Almighty knows when and how," he chattered as he walked towards the niche that he used as a cabinet.

"It's not Hastings," thought Bob annoyed with himself for getting caught up in irrelevant details.

"You haven't answered my question. Will you help me, or have you decided to try another ten appeals to the Archbishop for relocation?"

"Blair, you're late!" the minister answered in a completely different voice from the one that sent shivers down Bob's spine. "Your own personal guard came by looking for you three times. They may come back again. In any case, I prepared what is needed though I did not know if you would return."

Blair realized that they were not alone. An old woman sat on a sack that Blair somehow knew to be full of dirty laundry. She gnawed some dried fruit. "This is Wilma," the minister said, the midwife who helped birth Anne Predator, *aka* Amaradaminda. I was lucky to find her. She moved ten years ago to Doylstone. She knows how to read and write, and she clearly noted Anne in her records, born at five in the morning on a Wednesday, May 1673, missing a rib. This should be all you need to proceed to the examination for the Devil's marks. But now it's your turn, Lord Blair. Time is getting short and tomorrow, on September 21st, this whole paradox that you are trying to solve will, in one way or another, come undone.

"So you know!" cried Bob, "My dear Professor Hastings, you knew it all the way! You can't imagine how glad I am not to be alone in this adventure!" But the old man's voice and tone had changed again; he began complaining of gout, the misdeeds of the administration, and the unfairness of the

Archbishop in Boston. Dawn peeked tentatively over the horizon as if time itself was asking for a respite.

Blair woke as if from an uneasy sleep, drank the water from the mug on the nightstand, and pulled the sheet over his head as if it were a shroud that could not quite cover his whole body. He saw the lamp still on and the mud he had tracked onto the light blue carpet in the bedroom. He thought about getting out of bed and getting an aspirin or an Alka-Seltzer, the best cure for the flu. He smelled the aroma of the coffee he had made the night before when, having come in exhausted and wet to the bone, he had thought of drinking it in bed, with a drop of cognac, before going to sleep.

He didn't do any of these things, however. Instead he walked toward the old woman who bowed deeply at seeing the medallion inscribed with his rank, with the result that she scattered uneaten fruits around her..

"I will say whatever Your Highness wanted me to say!" she mumbled, trying desperately to catch the minister's eye. Bob looked at her with pity. It's a good thing we got to her before the sheriff's men, he thought.

"You will go with me," he answered her. "And all you will have to say is the truth: always only the truth."

Heavy steps in the yard. Then, a deafening knock that threatened to break down the door interrupted the conversation.

"You'll come with me as well, right?" Blair managed to ask the minister.

"I'll come. If for nothing else, at least for that *claviceps pur-*

purea."

"It's more than that," Blair added calmly. "You'll be dead in ten months..."

"Amen!" agreed the minister. "Maybe now you finally understand the only relocation I've ever asked for."

The guards burst into the room driving away all doubts with the brightness of their torches. "The charter from London has not arrived yet, Lord Blair," the head officer said, "and the mayor and sheriff ask that you please start the trial as soon as possible."

Dawn suddenly broke through on the morning of September 21, 1692. Invigorated by the light, Blair felt master of everything. "The minister and the old woman are coming with us. Let the Council meet immediately."

"Very well," answered the officer. "They are waiting for you impatiently. Without the charter, the people have once again begun to grumble, and the mayor didn't know where to find you."

"I've been investigating details, something that you are probably no longer used to around here. It's no wonder that there are so many irregularities!"

The officer bowed in embarrassment.

"Tell Master Harley to take care of the mob. I don't want to see him inside the court room under any circumstances. He is much too devoted to be unmasked now. We will need him again, especially once the charter arrives. I will hold you personally responsible for this."

Flattered by Lord Blair's faith in him, the officer agreed

immediately

"Please escort the minister and this woman to the Council with the utmost secrecy. No one is to speak to them until we begin the proceedings. This is of major importance, and any defiance will be reported directly to London!"

As soon as he uttered these words, the room began spinning around him. As if through fog, he saw the old woman and Professor Hastings being led away. He saw himself searching guiltily under the minister's bed where he eventually found a paper on Harvard University letterhead granting *Professor Emeritus* status, which he tried to burn in the fading coals of the stove.

He sensed the smell of the coffee again. He knew that he had left the coffee maker on when, wet and tired, he had gone to bed, but could not help thinking that maybe Carol had come back in the meantime, and there would be a real breakfast waiting for him downstairs as it had in those days when the children were young and everything seemed to be perfectly normal. Maybe it was not too late; maybe this time he would be able to talk to her. Sometimes things have a way of working themselves out just when all hope seems to be gone.

He got up from his bed, but the muddy boots, heavy beard, and medallion made him give up all illusions. He gave one last, nostalgic look to the Whistler reproduction above the Venetian mirror, *The Marina at Deauville: Harmony in White and White.*

A soldier from his guard escorted him with equal parts docility and insolence. He reached the imposing building of the Council at eight sharp on the morning of September 21, 1692.

He was undressed right away, with devotion but also urgency, by two of the mayor's assistants. He noticed the smell: musty clothes mixed with sweat. The starched white collar, black robe and cape of the judges of the British Empire were placed on his unresisting body like an armor, while in the big room of the Council House, a seemingly castrated usher announced in his soprano voice: "Hear ye! Hear ye!Lord Blair is here!"

He smelled the coffee one last time, saw the trees on the west side of Fifth Avenue out the bedroom window, and yelled in vain, "Carol! Carol!" then "Myra, Myra, is this you, finally?" After a while, after the emptiness became more and more apparent, he added: "Daniel, now I know. At least you no longer have to be a judge."

There was no answer to any of this. He stopped impotently in front of Whistler's marina where, all of a sudden, he could see Amy running and looking extremely dramatic, while prominently displaying the sapphire crucifix on its half gold, half silver chain. He writhed in bed and the sheet that had previously been a shroud now felt like a womb pulsating painfully around him. The pulses became more and more frequent and the birth pains that he felt all the way into his bones threatened to expel him. He woke up mumbling, "My God, I didn't know how painful it is to be born!"

"Hear ye! Hear ye! Lord Blair presides," continued the usher, and Bob, clad in all the attributes of his rank, walked into the bright court room from which there was no return.

The funeral home *Proctor & Barth* on Madison Avenue has a chapel used solely for memorial services. In the case of Robert Blair, this was the most appropriate option. He had disappeared without a trace one day, and all the police investigations, including those of the FBI, had come up empty. His bedroom was untouched with the bed still made, and Carol's statements had been fairly useless as she had not been home in two weeks.

Phil McCormick had taken care of all the arrangements. A Phil as few had seen in the last few years—sober, elegant, quiet, perfectly awake, and unspeakably sad. He had paid for the entire service as well as the printing of the invitations that had been sent to the entire gang of alumni, Harvard Law class of '72. All had come except for Marlon who, in typical fashion, said, "I bet he's upstate hunting ghosts again and we're all going to sit there like idiots crying in front of an empty coffin. Only a dolt like McCormick could come up with something like this. It seems that sobering up doesn't agree with him. It makes him even more of what he always was—an idiot!"

Phil, however, suspected that Harley did not attend because he was afraid. For a long time after this incident his house in Westchester was kept under heavy guard with uniformed security, and he stopped inviting all sorts of illustrious celebrities to his crazy parties as he once had.

"Organ music always makes me feel guilty. I feel like crying," whispered Brad Wilkins to Winkler who had gotten a leave from Amerhurst for the day. They had been the best of friends in college, and only Johnny's illness had kept them apart lately.

"Very well," answered Winkler gently. "If you feel like crying then that is what you are supposed to do. There's no point in fighting it. Besides this is the most appropriate time and place for such things," he added with a smile.

Brad did in fact cry quietly, or rather, he let the tears pour down his cheeks. "I don't know. It's more than that, perhaps," he said after a time. "You see, Bobby had divulged a series of things to me that ... In any case, they're not simple or easy to explain. I think that if I had done something then, maybe only just stayed with him for a while, it would have prevented..."

"His disappearance?" asked Winkler. "No way! He did not disappear outwardly, but inwardly."

"So you don't think he's dead! Tell me, do you really know anything concrete about this?"

"Brad, Brad! Same old Brad! There are certain things about which you cannot say you *know* or don't *know* anything without demonstrating a complete misunderstanding of them. Bob spoke to me too, perhaps in the same terms as to you. But if you feel any guilt, it should not be about this inevitable situation. You should set your mind at ease on that count. If there's anything to feel guilty about, it may be the incredulous attitude with which you met his confession. You thought he had gone nuts, right?"

"To tell you the truth," answered Wilkins relieved, "I never used such strong terms, and I certainly never said anything to

· 138 ·

his face, but this makes me no less guilty of not having believed a word he told me. I told him to relax, take some time off, go to Vermont (the seaside is no good in situations of great stress) all in all to stop thinking so hard."

"Oh God, Brad! Go to Vermont?! As if our inner demons need to travel by train, plane, or car..."

"What was I supposed to say? The man was talking about three hundred year old witches, the trials that they endured, his own escapades in time travel and how, I don't remember where and when, he had to save his secretary, Amy, who, as you can well see, is still alive and perfectly fine and I don't even know if the FBI checked her out. Then he asked me for some obscure books and references that I used when writing my treatise on the nature of law and took feverish notes as if he was preparing to try a real case."

"Maybe that's exactly what he did, Brad! And the best proof is that we are here in his memory. It would be interesting to know if he managed to pay his debt to society. I mean what he thought of as his debt."

"See?" said Brad raising his voice. "Now you're starting to sound like him. Look Johnny, I never thought that you ... anyway, with all the medical evidence ... do you know what I'm trying to say?"

"Yes, yes. You're a good friend, Brad! You want to say that you never thought I was crazy, just, let's say ... gone to Vermont for a rest until the stress passes, right?

"Something like that," Wilkins agreed. "I too have changed lately, otherwise I wouldn't even think of asking you what I am about to ask. Do you really think that he got stuck *there*?"

"It's entirely possible," Winkler answered. "But it's just as possible that he never made it, and we'll find him tomorrow or the day after in his office, Amy will disappear as if she never existed, and we won't remember anything about this whole strange tale. It's also not impossible that he and Amy, or Amaradaminda, who, outside the confines of space and time is the same person, are floating around somewhere in the ether, hand in hand and soul in soul, pushed there by that most fearsome of Sires, the one that casts doubt onto the power of elevation. What can I tell you? Life is one infinite series of possibilities until death finds us and forces us to choose. Then, we begin to rise, each one as high as he can, leaving behind the illusion of our certainties for the one true reality from which we spring and to which we must return."

Brad looked around frightened. The organ music was howling above their heads and he felt something like an injured bird flapping desperately in the cavity between his heart and his stomach.

"John, you ... are you one of those ... wait a second, Bob told me about this sect..."

"You mean Gnostics, Brad?" an amused Winkler answered. "It's not a sect, and I'm surprised that, of all people, Bobby would tell you about such things. He must have loved you very much. You, the grand champion of rationalism. But then again, perhaps this is part of your initiation. You know, it would be no great insult to logic if you read the texts of Nag Hammadi. Collections of knowledge should never frighten a rational man, no matter how bold or unusual they are."

"I am ready to do anything to find Bob," answered Brad with determination. "I can't live with this guilt. It was clear that he would die from what he told me, and I did nothing to prevent his death. I wanted to confess, but I don't trust any of the ministers with this. So I ask you to please take my confession now and to give me whatever punishment you see fit. I'm ashamed that I have to come to you like this, but..." and the tears streamed down his face even though the organ stopped playing.

John Winkler put his head in his hands and shook a few times as if he was trying to cast off some particularly heavy burden.

"The cannon of the Rationalist, my dear, reborn Brad, is the neediest of all. For he constantly doubts without reason and believes fervently in that which is unbelievable. Remember the monstrous but superb phrase uttered by the famous Arnaud Amalric, I believe right before the destruction of Beziers or some other Cathar fortress, *"Tuéz les tous, Dieu reconnaîtra les Siens!"*[12] You will have to take off the armor of Rationalism, now so often pierced in battles worthy of a better champion, and replace it with the infinitely vulnerable cloak of lost illusions. So clad, I will dub you the Knight of Universal Deception and you will set off on the difficult and thankless road to spiritual redemption"

The chapel was dark. The cleaning staff had begun removing candelabra, and the only music to celebrate Brad's conver-

[12] "Kill them all, God will sort them out!"

sion was the sound of the vacuum cleaners going over the heavy carpet.

Two oldish men, walking slowly with their heads down came out of the chapel of the funeral home *Proctor & Barth*. They crossed Fifth Avenue and walked into Central Park at the corner of 70th Street.

"Brad," said Winkler after some time, "did you notice that Amy was wearing a sapphire cross around her neck today?"

"Yes," said Wilkins, "it could have been sapphire. I did notice that unusually large piece of jewelry. But what does that have to do with...?"

"It does!" said Winkler. "Because that is the cross that Anne Predator, *aka* Amaradaminda, wore before being hanged on September 22, 1692. One of the executioners tore it away from her throat because condemned witches were not allowed to wear the symbols of the church. You would probably know this better than me. You did after all work on all the ways in which justice was administered in the witch trials in Salem."

"Anne Predator," said Brad trying to remember. "She must have been one of the eight hanged at the order of Lord Ian Blair. Blair? Blair! You mean to say..."

"I don't mean to say anything. The obvious is always the most easily ignored. I'm sure you didn't notice, but the chain on which the cross hangs is half gold and half silver. It broke when it was torn away from Amaradaminda. Amy had it redone, but with silver instead of gold. She probably didn't have enough money. She got the cross from her mother, Amy, the daughter of another Amy, and the granddaughter and great granddaughter of a whole series of Amaradamindas that could only have been born if Bob reversed the 1692 decision. Lord Blair was one of his ancestors, as I'm sure is becoming clear. Just to be sure though, we must try another test, and you're the only one who can do it because I have to go back to the sanatorium tonight."

"I could arrange something, Johnny. You know, I do know some people and can muster up a bit of influence. I could get you out of there forever if you..."

"God forbid, Brad! I wouldn't give up my illness for anything! Don't disappoint me just now when I'm relying on you the most. You will need to go to Englewood, Massachusetts, to the old cemetery next to the water tower. If things are as I believe, you will find an old tombstone with Amaradaminda's name, or probably Anne Predator's. This is your first trial as the newly dubbed Knight of Universal Deception."

"That means," Wilkins said after thinking for a while, "that he's never coming back. And this Amy doesn't even know what he has done for her! It's repulsive, Johnny, a stupid girl, a nobody, who just lives from day to day, while Bob..."

"You're saying this? You're the one who wrote an entire treatise on the spirit of justice where you proved that we are all equal in the eyes of the law no matter how beautiful, ugly, smart, or idiotic we are. As long as we know that Bob is there because of her, things make some sense. He will certainly reverse the other seven sentences as well, and not because there are no witches, but because those women, like Amaradaminda, were unjustly hanged." Brad's eyes shone as if with a new light.

POST-SCRIPTUM

My Dear Johnny,
I found the grave. The tombstone is half buried in the ground. I could barely distinguish the writing on the worn stone. I transcribe exactly what I read with my own eyes:

Anne Predator aka Amaradaminda, 1673-1729
Mourned by her husband, Gilbert, and six inconsolable children
Requiesquat in Pacem!

Excuse me for not writing sooner, but once I got back to New York I began a detailed study of the cases of the other seven victims of September 22, 1692. It's extremely tedious, but I have more energy than I did when I was young. The grave of Margaret Smithe, another of the women hanged on the same day as Amaradaminda, has appeared out of nowhere in the cemetery at Brisbane, near Englewood. The old minister who showed it to me swears that it had never been there, never! That is, not until now, when we could both see it clearly.

Presumably Bob is working tirelessly. I must confess that I am too. I don't sleep at all anymore, but I'm happier than ever. I've started reading some things about ... you know better than me, what I used to call a sect. And now, as soon as the new edition of my treatise on the nature of law comes out, I can only hope that you will reserve a spot for me next to yourself, because I'm coming soon!

Yours in fraternity,
Brad Wilkins,
The Knight of Universal Deception

PPS. I saw Amy yesterday. The chain is whole and all gold again!

PANIC SYNDROME!

U pon understanding nothing and realizing that all medical tests—so minute, costly and, often, humiliating—were useless, I decided to consider myself rather *healthy* and, maybe, as Voltaire says, happy, because this has a beneficial influence on the organism. But it didn't have. This much was obvious: I was subject to a general malaise that I could not control in any way, and all its miseries—now itemized in detail—were recurring more or less periodically, I'd say—"out of the blue." It was then that I resolved to abandon the ways of general medicine—which had declared me healthy beyond doubt—and to have recourse to psychiatrists and psychoanalysts that, praise the Lord, come in sufficient numbers here. I transcribe only a few crucial encounters of mine with a domain that, even if it proved incapable of fixing me, occasioned some exquisite revelations.

March 12, 1993
"You will agree, Dr. Goldenberg, that if this ... this chronic anxiety, this panic syndrome, or whatever else you'd want to call it, had been discovered by Romanians, it would've been called *moft*."

Everything was alright, so far, but how could I get across to Dr. Goldenberg, indisputably, a famous authority, the meaning of the word *moft*. I tried, to the best of my humble abilities, to translate from Caragiale's Romanian its rough meaning. But when I reached the passage where Caragiale writes:

"*The Patient* (very impatiently): Doctor, I am dying!

The Doctor (very calmly): *Mofts*!", it seemed that I kind of touched a chord.

"Hm, yeah!" says he. "This doctor of yours must've had a pretty solid malpractice insurance to allow himself to deny a patient the natural right to suffer from something. Because what I get from what you have told me, although all the symptoms you mentioned here (*joys and sorrows, merit and infamy, guilt and happenings, right, duty, feelings, interests, convictions, politics, black plague, languor, diphtheria, Sybaritism, destructive vices, suffering, misery, talent and imbecility, moon- and mind-eclipses, past, present, and future* —quoted from Caragiale) don't seem to have much to do with our case—it will hurt the patient more than it will soothe him, vexing him and noticeably increasing his *anxiety*. Whether this anxiety is real or imagined, is not our business! Look what he did to you. Had he cured you, you would not be sitting in my office right now. However, give me a moment to take a few notes from your doctor's case ... Not that it would have any scientific value—the guy is unquestionably a dilettante—but it might be of use in an article of mine which should appear without fail in ..., and which denounces precisely such unfitting attitudes toward a patient that—well, since he has the means, and wishes to subject himself to treatment that is often costly—should not be discouraged! Maybe you can recall some other things he told you when he used this ridiculous concept ... as you said, *moft*, with regard to your wholly justified disorder that we'll try right away to cure."

"No, you didn't get me right," I smiled, as I often do in America. "Mr. Caragiale was not my doctor ... let's say, not in the sense in which you think. He died in 1912, in Berlin."

"Aha, that's interesting! Did he have any connection with the psychomotric circle of Schulemberg?"

And he was feverishly taking notes, writing all the time (in a jittery and large handwriting) on a (large) pad. I had brought a little notebook in which I would write nothing, neither then, nor later.

"You see, Dr. Goldenberg, Caragiale was not a doctor. He is a classic Romanian writer, whom I reread now and then, although, practically, I know his stuff by heart. And, then, he died in 1912, how could I have met him otherwise than, say, in spirit—which, I have to admit, as you have said, wouldn't have much to do with our case!"

"Alright, alright..." said Dr. Goldenberg, clearly disappointed. "We don't deal here with these kind of problems ... I mean temporal ones. As you said, there might well be a chronological conflict—he did not consult you personally—but this does not mean much for medical practice in general; for, in diagnosing this as a *moft*, he has actually acting like a doctor: like a bad one, I must say, who minimizes suffering and seeks, God knows out of what reckless, cynical, or altruistic tendency—it is all the same—to discourage the sacred duty to develop a complex, long-term treatment, based on clear prescriptions and on following up on the case with the purpose of

... well, the amelioration of the symptoms and, perhaps, the total elimination of the ailment, in due time!"

"But, Dr. Goldenberg, all these are criteria that you may follow in your common practice ... Caragiale, well, he can't be subjected to such standards ... It was more of a parenthesis with which I was trying to show how Romanians would regard such a, let's call it leisurely illness, where the patient is physically healthy...."

"Well-well, my dear friend, not quite! And stop looking at your watch. It won't cost you more than one session at the price that ... well, you know it already ... We might as well extend this discussion a bit, and I hope you won't mind if I take some more notes ... you know, for my article, because it seems that this individual had certain intuitions which, albeit totally unsuitable, are extremely interesting!"

"And how about me? When are we going to talk about my case proper?"

"But this is exactly what we're doing ... all the while! Don't worry! Tell me more about him; this will help us understand, perhaps, the hidden aspects of the disease, those aspects that are less evident at first sight. In any case, it is clear that you could not possibly have consulted him personally ... but what other diagnoses of his are known?"

Poor Caragiale! I thought. He hasn't even been an adherent to Schulemberg's psychomotric group in his Berlin years. What's more, time goes by and I hadn't even had a chance to explain anything of what bothers me!

"In principle, I'd say that his *diagnoses*, if you want to call them this, were referring to all of us living over there, in the old country...."

"Hm, wellll!" He retorts while scribbling feverishly. "An endemic disease."

"No, Doctor Goldenberg, you make it sound as if it were a case of *Thalassemia,* I sort of know something about these matters, too ... I come from a family of doctors."

"This makes things even worse! Hodgepodge knowledge only brings about more confusion... such shards of knowledge are, you must realize, rather useless fragments. And I hope you'll agree with me when I say that nothing is more harmful than partial expertise ... This, of course, from a perspective that is—you have enough background to understand—*holistic*! Look, don't take it personally, but you should forget everything you knew beforehand, or, the treatment that I would attempt to develop for your case might fail! It seems that you've got a prime obsession with the theories of this quack you keep talking about. Analyzing his thinking style, we will succeed in determining with clarity that *nexus* which, while acting at the level of the mind, affects your, medically-speaking, otherwise perfect physical state!"

Well, here my doctor seemed to strike closer to home.

"Well," I said, "Dr. Goldenberg, if, for instance, someone were to say the word *cleanly* to you, what would you add to it?"

I thought that this time I had really cornered him. Dr. Goldenberg took his glasses off, pinched his nose a few times, and then shot off:

"Cleanly, that is to say, spotless, let's say, immaculate,

morally flawless, hygienic..."

"You see, somewhere he writes *cleanly dirty*; d'you get it? Maybe this doesn't have anything to do with either the *moft* or my sickness that we haven't had time to talk about, but this is what he says, and we, those from over there, seem to be somehow condemned to this, let's call it, *oxymoron*. So much so, that no one there can say *cleanly* without immediately adding, or at least thinking, maybe involuntarily: *dirty*!"

"Aha! *Cyclothymic*! Very interesting!"

"Not quite. In general, I've been categorized as either a *schizoid* or, on the contrary, a *paranoid*, but never as a *cyclothymic*."

"No, I wasn't talking about you, this is secondary right now ... Him! It's him I'm talking about, the one who is the source of your obsessions ... This Caragiale! He must have been a *cyclothymic*, do you understand? *Cleanly dirty*, this is a typical example! Look, for the time being you must take these pills ... let's see how they work, and then, to the extent that the symptoms will, you see...? But first and foremost, avoid any form of stress, this is crucial ... Things are going on the right track," he said, and tidied up for the nth time all the objects on his table—had been doing this for almost the entire duration of the time he spent talking to me—so that none of them would be out of line or protruding beyond the edge of the table. "Ah, as to this Car ... well, whatever you called him, I urge you, don't even think of reading from him again. Otherwise the drugs I gave you won't have any effect ... And they are expensive enough! And, in general, leave aside the books ... Total *relax-*

ation, as much *relaxation* as possible," said he while picking his nose, and inquisitively examining the finds.

I couldn't get out of there soon enough. All of a sudden I felt healthy and in no need of any help whatsoever. How the hell had I gotten here? I swore to myself to never in my life set foot in such a doctor's office!

"Ah," said Dr. Goldenberg as I was about to leave. "One more thing ... Maybe it's trivial, but it interests me—for my article, you know, the one for the *New England Review of Medical Science*. When you are on a bridge or somewhere, in a very high place, do you ever feel like spitting in the water, or spitting down? Don't think, just answer as quickly as you can, without any kind of auto-censorship!"

"I don't need to think at all," I said. "I always feel like spitting, and I actually do it when there is no one around!"

"Heh, he," Dr. Goldenberg laughed meaningfully and, for a moment, he stopped taking notes. "I do the same! Isn't that something?"

V

"I feel like sleeping when I am supposed to be awake. I can't sleep when I would like to. In the morning I wake up more tired than when I went to bed, and my heart beats sometimes too fast and irregularly, other times almost imperceptibly, as if I were about to breathe my last breath. In such moments, as if these weren't enough, it suddenly seems to me that my finger-nails grow uncommonly fast, and my beard too, oh, Lord, sometimes I feel almost like I am dead .... But, no! Right away, my heart starts going crazy, hands and feet grow numb, I have vertigo, and a sensation of choking or suffocating because of the lack of air: that makes me breathe fast, like a fish out of water. Then I get even dizzier, I am about to faint, and can't think of anything else but that "I feel enormously and see monstrously." It must be these pills! I'll try to get rid of them right away. But how? You see, Dr. Lieberman, that's why it's not good to swear: I had sworn to never again set foot in such a doctor's office ... And here I am now!"

"You did exactly what you had to do," said Dr. Lieberman kindly. "As to these spells, however outlandish and unbearable they might seem to you, they don't represent the slightest danger for you, even if—and I do understand this—it is hard for you to believe!"

"I hope you don't doubt that I feel ill ... by the way, I think it's written there, too, in the papers from Dr. Goldenberg...."

"Not at all," smiled Dr. Lieberman. "It is normal to feel bad since you follow a treatment that is absolutely inadequate for your ailment...."

"Thank you," I said, obviously reassured. "Thanks a lot ... At least, I hope the world won't think I'm crazy!"

"Crazy? Oh, dear man, how can you say such a thing? And especially here, in my office, to me who has demonstrated in so many books and throughout my entire medical career that there is no such thing as mad people. Have you ever met one? Of course not ... All of these states of yours are induced by those pills...."

"Alright, alright," I said, "But I wasn't feeling well before taking them either, this is why I went to see Dr. Goldenberg..."

"This is a different problem altogether. We'll get to it in due time, no question about that. Lissy—this is what we call Dr. Goldenberg—is a sweetie, I hope you'll agree...! But this is how he is: he examines you very carefully, both psychologically and intellectually, this is his well-known theory, after which he prescribes pills right away. Oh, well, maybe this is just the thing in some cases; you know, our discipline is more of an art. However, in your case I would never have prescribed pills, neither those nor any others. Anyway, it is clear that all of Lissy's observations—which we'll make an extensive use of—isn't he absolutely adorable with his obsessive way of asking you if you spit from a high place?—lead doubtlessly to a treatment based exclusively on behavioural self-control and exercises in desensitization!"

"Absolutely, Dr. Lieberman. I can't stand pills, particularly the ones I am taking now. But do you think that this treatment will work? This ... this behavioural desensitization?"

"Without a shadow of a doubt ... your mistake is that you create far too many problems for yourself ... Look, this is precisely what Lissy writes here, too, in his case ... It seems that it all started with the obsessive compulsion you have for a kind of a *guru* ... after all, things like this happen, especially here ... we live in a city which is a haven for all sorts of beliefs, one weirder than the other, and for hundreds of charlatans that stick ideas into people's heads, and empty their pockets...."

"You are referring to *Caragiale*," I dared to say, hoping, though, that it wasn't the case.

"Exactly," nodded Dr. Lieberman. "I didn't dare to pronounce such a name which is ... which is so uncommon. In any case, I must warn you that it might not even be his real name. Most of the time these so-called *gurus* or occasional *healers* more often than not take on false names, generic pseudonyms. Dr. Goldenberg notes here clearly that you reread him often, although you know him almost by heart ... It is like a *mantra* for you, as far as I can tell ... Such rituals may very well be widespread in the culture of your country of origin, where people, gathered together, repeat syllables, words, or sentences, hours on end. But I hope you realize that in our case such practice does nothing else than throw you into a confused state, so that your body—which, according to the very detailed tests you took, is perfectly healthy—reacts in the most normal possible way: all it does is defend you. The panic, the anxieties you complain of, are precisely the vigorous reaction of your organism: an entirely benign symptom that warns us against certain behavioural deviations that go against nature."

"Such as, for instance, reading Caragiale?" I asked.

"But of course! You see, Lissy was partially right, we face a *compulsive maniacal syndrome with a derivative fixation*.... This Caragiale, you mention his name all the time, better disappear from your life for good. If you want the treatment that I think of prescribing to you to work, you should stop seeing him, reading his teachings, and thinking of his *mantras*. I see here one of the *adversative-obsessional* types that you mention all the time: *cleanly-dirty*, and, all in all, I'd like you to consider him a dead man!"

"That's just what he is, Dr. Lieberman. He died in Berlin, in 1912, and had no connections with Schulemberg's psychomotric school!"

"Ah, he's dead?" asked Dr. Lieberman intrigued. "Lissy does not mention this here." And she, too, started taking notes on a pad. "Hmm ... things seem to be getting more complicated ... Do you, by any chance, have encounters with him, do you hear voices or, well, other phenomena...."

I felt that I was about to explode. Oh, *les misérables*!

"Dr. Lieberman," I said in a tone maybe a tad too rash, and then somewhat raising my voice, "I beg you to leave Caragiale in peace. He's never been—neither when I went to Dr. Goldenberg (or Lissy, as you call him, although I think that a name like this is more for a dog or a cat), nor now, when I hoped to finally get adequate treatment—anything else but a simple *parenthetical example*. A rather expensive one, since it has cost me more than three hundred dollars, and I see that not even today will I get by any cheaper, or end up more healed..."

"Relax ... relax!" smiled Dr. Lieberman, "I won't mention him again ... if this bothers you so much. Look, in our medical practice which, I think I told you, is more of an art, sometimes mistakes happen, too; mistakes that result from premises assumed in a way that is, let's say, inadequate. As did, for instance, Dr. Goldenberg, Lissy, despite his indisputable competence ... Sure, he was completely off the mark when he centred the discussion on this topic—I promised you I would not pronounce his name anymore, didn't I!—instead of dealing in fact with your own case. And the pills that he prescribed you ... as I said, seem to be completely inadequate in your case...."

It was obvious by now that Dr. Lieberman was a completely different kind of psychiatrist. All of a sudden I felt relaxed, confident, radiant.

"However, you must agree," she added, "that someone who says or thinks *cleanly-dirty, cleanly-dirty* all the time, can't be feeling quite well ... I mean it's not normal. Now, what you want—and what you must regain—is precisely your natural ease, your calm, uncramped state. For instance, stretch your legs, put your feet on the table, don't worry, and try to *relax!*"

I tried and it was dreadful: my feet on the table, my butt about to fall off the chair, my neck—stiff, a dull and piercing pain in my nape, maybe because the chair was too far from the table, or maybe because, in principle, I detest putting my feet on the table....

"Hey," exulted Dr. Lieberman, "isn't it better?"

"No," I answered relieved, since she had asked, anyway. "My legs and arms tingle, as if I'd slept on them, plus this pain between my shoulders." I didn't even mention the butt.

"Perfect!" she said. "Now, let's resume your initial position. This only confirms the fact, which I proved eloquently in some older works of mine, that, in the end, we all have our own ways of *relaxing*. Yours is a bit uncommon: you don't relax with your feet on the table ... As to the tingling, it is caused by the pills prescribed by Dr. Goldenberg, a treatment, to be sure, most proper for certain *exogenous* cases, while you happen to suffer from an *endogenous* syndrome. Would you be so good and take off your trousers?"

"No way!" I answered, glancing instinctively at the door.

"I thought so," said Dr. Lieberman with a wide smile, taking notes again. "It is totally normal not to want to expose oneself, to feel the desire for privacy. However, this needn't obsess you!"

"But who said I was obsessed? Moreover, I don't see what my disease has to do with..."

"It has, quite a lot, if you look at things from a *holistic* perspective, if you know what I mean. We'll get to this, too, give it some time. For the time being, let us try the desensitization exercises ... Look, imagine you are not feeling well, that you have one of those crises: your heartbeats are now too fast, now too slow, you feel like you are choking, that you can't breathe anymore, that you'll either faint or lose your mind ... Like this ... Close your eyes, *relax*, and imagine your favourite landscape ... Stay there, rest there for a few minutes, analyse closely each detail of the landscape, oh! ah! how *relaxing* ... You see? Where are the heartbeats, the suffocation, the dizziness? They are completely gone! This is what we'll be doing for some time," said Dr. Lieberman opening her eyes as if returning from a trance in which God knows what she saw ... "Alright, close your eyes and let's start!"

I closed my eyes, pressing my eyelids shut as best I could, not seeing anything, proded on and on by her voice: "Good. Just like this ... we're doing very well!"

"I've got a problem!" I said, opening my eyes precisely

when Dr. Lieberman was probably thinking that I was doing really well. "I don't have a favourite landscape ... I am not prepared, I never thought about it!"

"This is insignificant," she said a bit piqued, "you are an intelligent man, imagine anything ... anything that would really please you ... Come on, try it ... I think we are on the right track!"

I closed my eyes again, while I was receiving indications like: "No, no, no! Your eyelids are closed too tight, this is not a sign of *relaxation*, let your head fall backwards, like this ... don't move your fingers, your hands must be feeling light, in a *relaxed* position ... Can you please tell me now what you see?"

"Herds of unicorns ... herds of unicorns bathing in the sea...."

"Hmm!" she said, "are you sure that *this* is your favourite scenery?"

"Absolutely!" I answered. "Only that the noise of the sea and all their frolicking induce in me, I really don't want to say it ... a kind of *panic*!"

"Feel free to cut off the sound"—and she looked at her watch—"in fact, a landscape doesn't always have to have sound. On the contrary, it is even more *relaxing* if you don't hear a thing. We will try this for a few weeks, and you will see that everything will go really well."

VI

"And, did it?" asked Dr. Reichbar not without a hint of irony.

"Not at all! Had it worked, would I have come to your office? In three weeks, all I found out was that I hated my favourite landscape with all my heart! You know, associating it all the time with my worst states ... Maybe it was partially my fault, too, because I could never cut off the sound."

"You aren't guilty in the least," said the doctor, who had green, very intense eyes, and an extremely pleasant voice. "Why don't you call me Debra ... we'll have to go a long, long way ... together! The treatments that my colleagues—to call them such—prescribed in your case are, simply, aberrant: *placebo*, if you know by any chance what this means...."

"That is a kind of bull," I exclaimed.

"Precisely!" she allowed. "Here, at our therapy centre, we regard such ailments from an entirely distinct perspective ... I'll give you a few brochures to read ... They will help you along the long road we will cover together! It's a perspective that doesn't leave anything to chance, and that comprises, how should I put it, everything...."

"*Holistic*," I said, inspired by the recently acquired wisdom.

"Yes," said Debra, "you can call it *holistic*, and it is good for you to be aware of this. For instance, you know that each thing, endowed with life or not, is an extraordinary source of energy, an immense permanent explosion that we can't see or feel only because of the perversion of our senses, a phenomenon that allopathic medicine has all but increased by resorting to drugs, psycho-physical speculations, and other things like that ... Look what state they brought you to!"

"But, Debra, I was sick before I went to see Dr. Goldenberg and Dr. Lieberman. This, at least, is written in black on white, in all the papers in the file...."

"This is precisely the problem! This file does not interest us at all! We won't even open it! For, my friend, *there are no sick people*, this is an illusion maintained by ... you know ... you easily realize why ... There are only *energies*, which may be either positive or negative. Do you understand? It's very simple: in your case the negative energies probably prevail over the positive ones. All we have to do is *balance* them properly, and everything will be ex-cell-ent!"

She was blinking fast, with her beautiful and intense eyes, and for a moment she seemed extremely convincing. But then, suddenly:

"Take off all your clothes and I will try to decipher the exact nature of the energies!"

I thought at once that she was probably conniving with the other one, Dr. Lieberman, but the fact that she had not opened the file (where, in all likelihood, it was written that I have an aversion to intimacy!) made me abandon the idea. I was feeling very well again, no longer afraid of my bizarre states, and all I wanted at that moment was to leave the place as soon as possible.

"But couldn't one survey these energies ... through my clothes?"

"By no means!" she said. "The epidermis develops an *aura* that the clothes constantly obstruct ... This is, in fact, one of the most innovative points brought forth in my article published in the *Yale Journal of Medical Practice*: to feel better, we should walk around naked, untainted by any touch. But, you see, social pressure, wherefrom so many misfortunes come, forces this sense of humiliation upon us ... so conventional, and so damaging. Look, here is a hallstand, I'll go to the other room to *relax* in order for the consultation to succeed."

I took off my clothes, then I laid face down on the table.

Dr. Reichbar did not take long.

"*Relax*," she told me with her seductive voice. "Tenseness is a hypostasis characteristic of the dressed body."

Instinctively, I looked over my shoulder, terrified that she had *relaxed* too much, but no, she was fully dressed, eyes closed, moving her hands up and down above by back. From time to time she would murmur: "Ah! dizzy spells, well, no wonder, here I sense a very bad pressure point," or "Hum, it's clear that you don't like pats on the shoulder! I don't blame you for that ... But, lower ... very bad energies, the coccigian zone, this is to be kept in mind, try to wear briefs without elastic ... this might help!"

I was sweating alright, although it was not very warm in the office. I had hoped that, once she had gotten to the *coccis*, the examination would come to an end, when, all of a sudden, without opening her eyes, Debra said:

"Now turn on your back, we will examine the abdominal energies!"

"Couldn't one read the abdominal energies from this side ... I am kind of weak, with a bit of *relaxation* ... maybe...."

"No way!" Debra whispered, and turned me, briskly, in the desired position.

Again she moved her hands above me, murmuring: "Your body talks to me... it tells me very clearly that you do not eat properly, hence the dizzy spells, the heartbeats and all the rest ... You should eat more ... colourful! I am not sure ... Ah, yes! Something between yellow and red...."

"Orange," I tried "... oranges!"

"Hum... Yes, maybe orange... but not oranges. Their energies are mixed... Carrots, as many carrots as possible, and rice!"

"But the rice isn't orange!" I protested vehemently, maybe because I can't stand rice.

"It doesn't matter," Debra went on, "rice with carrots... this is what your body tells me it would like, to balance the negative energies!"

She then started palpating my arms, going up the neck.

"Green!" she said in the end, without opening her eyes "... Green ... Your body told me that you have to dress in green ... or, wait a second, at least the sleeves should be green ... You understand that, if we can't walk around naked as in fact we should, at least we should wear what our body tolerates best! Now you can get dressed! But you must come back weekly for check-ups."

After I got dressed and sort of got hold of my senses, she asked me, blinking again with her aquamarine eyes:

"Now, don't you feel a lot better?"

"Certainly," I had to acquiesce, "especially in comparison with...."

"No!" said Debra, "don't even mention comparison! This ruins it all. We will go on with the *epidermic* communication until you reach absolute *relaxation*, the natural state in which you must always find yourself. Trust me, I've succeeded with so many patients, after all ... I can give you addresses and phone numbers if you want ... Bye-bye, bye-bye, see you next week!"

I was giddy when I left. I must confess that, while I don't have a penchant for carrots and I hate rice, also I don't find green clothes particularly becoming, or, at least, not with a figure like mine. I went, nevertheless, to the *Banana Republic* across the street, and I bought myself a verdant shirt and green pyjamas. I wore them for a while, until my little girl started calling me *Froggy*. As to the carrots with rice, they gave me nothing more than terrible constipation, which provided anything but *relaxation* ... At least, I had not set foot again in Debra's office for the weekly *epidermics*. Even so, the first one cost enough, and the diagnosis she gave me (for she does not believe in diseases or sick people) did not even give me a chance to get my money back from the medical insurance ... As to the crises: they went on all the same—heartbeats, suffocation, the sensation that I am losing my mind....

VII

"Frankly, it amazes me that you are still able to function normally, and to do your job at the university!" exclaimed the Professor, Dr. Kaplan, understandingly. "You must have an iron will. How do you manage during the crises?"

"Like I know?" I answered. "Now and then, I take a pill from those left from Dr. Goldenberg, sometimes I close my eyes and contemplate the unicorns bathing in the sea, or I touch, from time to time, a green sleeve, munch on a carrot, or gulp down a bowl of boiled rice. What can I do? Probably this *holistics* stuff does not agree with me at all...."

" *Holistics, Schmolistics!"* Dr. Kaplan laughed condescendingly. "What is *holistics* after all, but a collection of *fragments*. You do realize now, I hope, that it is them we have to focus on!"

"Yes, yes, doctor. For instance, this disease, my ailment is, certainly, a fragment that deserves all the attention... after all, this is why I am here!"

Prof. Dr. Kaplan had an respectable baldness and a pair of small, inquisitive, and extremely lively eyes.

"Let's not rush into things!" he said, raising his right index finger solemnly. "First and foremost, it is known that constipation *per se* can induce dizziness, suffocation and all the rest... It is an anomalous state, you must admit, that we will have to eliminate first!"

"Then, please, remember"—I grew angry—"that I had these symptoms even before the *epidermics*, the rice, the carrots, dressing in green, and everything else, such as the

Goldenberg pills or the unicorns taking a bath in the sea. I did not come here because of a simple constipation! Look, read the file please, I hope that at least you will not ignore it, as did Dr. Reichbar!"

"Don't even mention it," Prof. Kaplan protested gently, "where this is concerned, you needn't worry. And that person you keep on calling *Doctor* Reichbar all but mocks the mission of our profession!"

Meticulously, he opened the file, examined each and every page, turned them over on each side, then arranged them in a new order and, although I must admit that everything he was doing could not but inspire confidence, in principle, I was becoming annoyed with this interminable rustle.

"Ah, it is crystal clear!" he then said, as if enlightened by the reading of those sheets in a different order. "Well, you suffer from a *phobia*, were you ever told this before? Look, if you put things head to head, they become clear all of a sudden. Phobias, my dear fellow, are compulsive behavioural disturbances, with a substratum... he! he! here we will have to do a bit of work, that is often hard to determine."

"Doctor, as I have had the honor of telling you, I suffered from all of these things before the rice, which, true enough, I detest ... still, a *phobia*...."

Dr. Kaplan took off his glasses and made a gesture of exasperation.

"But, my dear man, who said that you have a phobia of rice? No, it's an entirely different matter altogether. You have a phobia of this fellow, this Ca ... *Caragiale*, it's clear from your entire file. First you speak endlessly about him, then, all of a sudden, you can't stand him anymore, to the point where you even become violent and raise your voice when he is mentioned. Very interesting... but I wonder, whether what we have here is a rivalry, a misunderstood competition... maybe there's even a woman involved: in my recent studies I proved that phobias have, almost all of them, an erotic, sexual substratum!"

"'s dead!" I said, exasperated, and feeling like I was turning in circles.

"Who? *She* is? Under natural circumstances, I hope...."

"No, *he*, this unfortunate Caragiale."

"Oh, really? Let's see, is it written here? Where?...."

"In Berlin, in 1912," I managed to add, exhausted.

At this point, Dr. Kaplan ignored me completely, engrossed in reading the pages of my medical file, which, as I said, he kept arranging and rearranging.

"Interesting... very interesting... I gather from here that he was an obstinate opponent of Schulemberg, of the psychomotric school...."

"And, generally, of universal stupidity and foolishness," I caught myself murmuring.

"I fully agree!" said Dr. Kaplan, "Psychomotrism, really, was pure rubbish ... what I don't understand is where this phobia of yours comes from... because, no doubt, that's what causes all the bad moods of which you complain ... Anyway, you must promise me never to think about him again, in spite of all the theories and books which, out of a reflex to *rebound*, extremely frequent in cases of phobia, you feel drawn to read again and again....

I think I had grown so tired of trying so many times to clear up the misunderstanding with Caragiale, or maybe—I don't even know anymore—everything was so jumbled in my head, that sometimes I even believed, in all probability, that I truly suffered because of Caragiale! And so I let Dr. Kaplan go on as he pleased.

"We should, as a start," he said, "tackle that sexual, erotic aspect of the problem ... tell me, in this obsessive imagery that you keep developing, do the unicorns *go into* the sea or do they *come out*?"

"Obsessive imagery?" I protested. "But, Doctor, this is what Dr. Lieberman asked me to do...."

"No, no!" Prof. Kaplan contested. "She only told you to imagine your favorite scenery, you chose the elements yourself. Here is the most important thing!"

"I don't know ... I didn't think of this ... Generally, I think they're splashing about and making a terrible commotion, there, in the sea foam. Why is it so important whether they go in or out?"

"Aha! There's foam, too! It's clear, we must find out immediately whether they go *in*, because then we are faced with a complex produced by the incomplete satisfaction of the *libido*, whereas, if they are coming *out*, it's clearly the case of a *castration* complex! Please, close your eyes and try to record every detail with accuracy!"

What could I do? I closed my eyes half-heartedly:

"I can't tell you for sure, doctor, some of them go in, others come out, they're probably not all ready at the same time with... the bathing... by Jove, it's not the army!"

"Very well!" exclaimed Dr. Kaplan. "Now try to count the ones that are going in and the ones that are coming out, separately. Is there a lot of foam?"

"Pretty much! Like at the seaside..." I answered without opening my eyes. "Then, with all this horsing around, yes, there's a lot of foam...."

"Perfect, now count them!"

After a while I opened my eyes.

"I can't count them separately, doctor, because they're moving about constantly, and, then, all this counting is making me sleepy... I think they're in equal numbers or something like that...."

"Yes, yes! I expected as much, more or less," said Dr. Kaplan, taking notes. "Eroticism, therefore... frustrated libido, on the one hand, an incapacity for satisfaction... Tell me, please, do you practice masturbation?"

"Good grief, Doctor, I'm a married man, thank God, that's the last thing I need...."

"Married or not," Dr. Kaplan giggled, "it makes no difference here. On the contrary, I have been led to find so many times that this occurs especially with married people... You know, marriage—I, too, was married for thirty years—produces these habits, a certain apathy and the need to turn to... or to experiment with other sexual practices!"

I felt that I was losing my patience with this shrink, most

certainly perverse, since he kept shifting his half-closed eyes everywhere far too often, especially when he talked about eroticism and sex....

"But I love my wife, Doctor, I don't think that any of this has anything to do with the dizzy spells, the anxiety attacks, the palpitations, the suffocation and everything else. I have the feeling that we're digressing again, and that it has nothing whatsoever to do with my problem...."

"Ho, ho, ho!" laughed Dr. Kaplan hoarsely, "I hope you're not such a bigot or so narrow-minded to confuse sentiment with sex! But maybe you are, and then it's very clear why you're having these symptoms, let's call them *confusional*! Well, then let's recapitulate... the unicorns go into the sea and come out of the sea... foam is made... in, out, in, out... What more do you want than a typical instance of the sexual act?"

What a devil, this Doctor Kaplan! I sort of understood where he was heading, I was happy that he had at least left Caragiale in peace, but I still couldn't figure out what all this had to do with my moments of dizziness. After he had taken notes for a while, evidently satisfied with how things were unfolding, he slid his glasses down to the tip of his nose and said:

"It's clear what you must do! Every time you have a crisis, engage immediately in a sexual act! In time, this will take care of all your states, no doubt about it!"

"But," I protested, "they don't happen only at home ... Now that I think about it, they never happen at home!"

"You see? Where do they *happen*, so to speak, although I

know now that here nothing is happenstance!"

"Well," I said, "for example, in the subway, on my way to the university or on my way back, in a shop, at a reception, during a course, at a congress, on the street...."

"That's it, that's it!" Dr. Kaplan exulted. "Didn't I tell you? The unicorns going into the sea ... This is only because you want to have *them* all!"

"All what?" I asked stupidly.

"The *women*, it's them we're talking about! Don't you feel, sometimes, that you want to jump one, just like that, out of the blue?"

"No," I answered, sincerely ... I hope.

"Hum! I wouldn't say that ... the unicorns that go in and out, in and out! Heh, heh! You exposed yourself there, and from this we will also infer the basis of the treatment—it will be long, I want you to entertain no illusion about it—which we will prescribe! It's a typical syndrome of possession, which, because of social pressure, or anyway, because of the principles which you alone impose upon yourself, throw you into these most awful fits ... which you described so well: the dizziness, throbbing temples, feelings of suffocation and fainting!"

This time he had flummoxed me completely. I seemed to feel guilty about what I did do as well as about what I didn't do; especially since, all of a sudden, I was faced with the revelation that I might be an insatiable sexual monster....

"I would have never thought that I am some kind of repressed Casanova, or something like that ... as you see fit to insinuate, doctor!"

"But we, all of us, are like that! Ah, someday I'll tell you about myself... Anyway, maybe this is not the moment... Let's go back to the treatment: since you are unable to practice the sexual act in the, well, the above-mentioned circumstances, you will have to try to imagine it somehow ... Heh, heh! There are many ways of doing it, you will find the most appropriate one... This will relax you, without a doubt, and the crises will pass, miraculously, please trust me!"

Two weeks later, when I paid him another visit, I had to admit that I had had fewer crises. No wonder: I was too busy with something else. In the subway, when it seized me, I began to undress, in my mind, at random, a young thing sitting in the seat opposite to me, or maybe even two at a time, if my dizziness was too great, or if I felt that I was going to suffocate on the spot.

"Excellent idea!" Dr. Kaplan exclaimed, taking his usual notes. "I can actually prescribe this from now on in similar cases, with your permission."

"The only problem is, Doctor, that some of them get off too quickly and I don't have enough time to dress them back up, and then it happens that I also mix some of them up, so that one leaves stark naked, only with the other one's coat on, while the other one that stays on the train finds herself with two bras, two...."

"Their business! Their business!" said the doctor. "What's important is that you overcome the crisis and everything comes out perfectly! After all, you're really not responsible for the way in which people go about in New York ... Don't you dare, now that we've taken care of the erotic compulsion, develop a *guilt complex*, which is often the consequence in individuals with primitive moral principles."

"In this case," I decided, "I would rather go back to the image with the unicorns... at least it doesn't imply any sort of responsibility!"

"Who do you think you are, the Holy Ghost?" Prof. Kaplan grew annoyed. "Of course you have some sort of responsibility in all this, but you must face it like a man, you can't want to *possess them all* and then pretend nothing happened!"

"But, after all, nothing happens!" I protested. "And I don't want to possess them all either, as I had the honor of telling you; just like I didn't want the unicorns to go into the sea or to come out, in the treatment prescribed by Dr. Lieberman; just like I didn't want to strip buck naked for the *epidermics* performed by Dr. Reichbar, or to wear green, constipating myself with rice and carrots; just like I don't have any obsession with, or a phobia of Caragiale, who has never treated me, and who died in Berlin, without having, in all probability, anything to do with the psychomotric school of Schulemberg; and just like I have never felt like swallowing the pills of Dr. Goldenberg, or Lissy—dog, cat, whatever this guy may be, because the name is for anything but a human being! And, generally, I feel totally abused by your perverse way of making me undress all the women I happen to run into, without being then able to put all their things back on, and to decently let them go about their business...."

"Splendid, splendid!" sang out Dr. Kaplan. "Such a violent

reaction tells us more than we need, and this in a short amount of time ... in fact, very short ... Your illness is, as of now, almost healed, and you must realize that this can only make me happy, although I was hoping for a slower remission, which would allow me another series of sessions at the price which ... oh well, since the insurance is paying for it anyway.... "

"On the contrary!" I said, deep in thought. "It seems to me that now that I've gotten rid of one thing, I've acquired something even worse...."

"No, no!" said the doctor. "This shouldn't worry you! Didn't I heal you of dizziness, suffocation and everything else? What do you care that you'll be undressing women in your mind until the end of your days? Ah! I envy you: why didn't I hit upon this idea sooner! But ... perhaps you could reward me fittingly for the infallible treatment that I've prescribed for you: for example, you could at least bring me a bra ... you see, one of those that are left over; the women get in and out so quickly, I am well aware that you don't have enough time to put back everything that belongs to each one..." "Then," he continued heatedly, "you could try it with four or five women at a time, this would leave so many things left over... All you have to do is collect them, gently, after they get off the train, and bring them to me...."

VIII

"Unbelievable!" Dr. Finch marveled. "Are you sure that we're talking about Professor Kaplan?"

"Do you doubt it? Look, I even have his card, with the date of the last session, to which I didn't even go... The situation was getting worse and worse: I had the impression that it was me who was treating him!"

"Ah, I don't doubt it at all! It's clear that he suffers from a *somatic psychomania with an actant voyeuristic and equally fetishistic fixation* ... The symptoms are described in detail in one of his books ... You know, I was his student at Cornell... I wouldn't have suspected, however, that he is still... Nevertheless, here in your file, he says that you were able to materialize the erotic compulsion... a black bra is mentioned, which you gave him..."

"What could I do, Doctor Finch, he nagged me so much about it, that, in the end, I bought a bra and I took it to him... I told him that it was from one of the young girls in the sub-way...."

"Was he content?" asked the beautiful Dr. Finch, smoking absent-mindedly.

"Content is an understatement!" I answered her. "He was jumping around everywhere, stopping every now and then to take notes, after which he caressed the bra with long, lascivious strokes: 'Hum!! Perfect! What a scent!' There wasn't any scent, since I had bought it directly from Woolworth half an hour before!"

Dr. Finch put out her cigarette, took another look at the file, and then:

"Tell me again, why didn't you go to the last session?"

"Well, he asked me to bring him a pair of underwear, but I had sworn to myself, never to undress women again, no matter how sick I would feel, neither in the subway, nor at congresses ... nowhere ... It became clear to me that this preoccupation made my bad moments go away only because it shifted my attention on to something else, which, after all, could be quite captivating... But all the disorder that followed, with things that I couldn't put back on the persons... you understand... Furthermore, I thought that, after the underwear, the batty Prof. Kaplan would ask me to bring him Lord-only-knows what other thing ... a breast, or God forbid...."

"Of course I understand!" she purred. "You suffer from a *panic syndrome*, a widespread disorder in the last quarter of a century, especially here, in the States. The most effective treatment, although it is episodic, rather than long-term, is to shift the accent on to a preoccupation that would solicit your full attention: count money, do sports, or, why not? undress women ... This is not what intrigues me... I'm only thinking: I didn't know Prof. Kaplan would still want ...."

"Oh, no!" I got up, ready to leave as quickly as possible. "I'm sick and tired of talking about other people and their problems... I don't want to hear either about Caragiale, or about Goldenberg's pills, Lieberman's *relaxation* with unicorns, constipation with green sleeves *à la* Reichbar, or Prof. Kaplan's masturbations. I want to know about *myself*! *Me and only me*!"

"It's natural!" smiled Dr. Finch. The *panic syndrome* always reduces the individual to the self, in order for it then to actually make it clear to him that there's nothing else to do in the moments of crisis, except to find himself, like I said, a preoccupation outside of the self. The body is perfectly healthy, look, it's written here, all over the file, so you have nothing to fear: *mens sana in corpore sano!* You are perfectly healthy, but poor Kaplan, my good professor, doesn't he deserve to have a *preoccupation* as well? Didn't you think about his panic?"

"No!" I said firmly. "To hell with him."

"Come on, don't be so angry!" pleaded Dr. Finch, "Rony—that's what we, students, called Professor Kaplan—needs help more than anyone. I didn't suspect that he is still *active* at his age ... And since I don't really have captivating *preoccupations* either ... You understand me ... I would like you to do me a favor: look, the session won't cost you anything ... I'll just go over there and, be so kind, take my underwear to him ... Since you still have a session with him ... who knows?"

IX
April 11, 1997

"And did you take them to him?" asked Dr. Weichelt, "but it was clear that he had neither the perverse movement of Dr. Kaplan's eyes, nor Dr. Finch's frivolity, who, above and beyond the whole oddity with the underwear, at least gave me a somewhat more reasonable diagnosis.

"Not at all!" I answered. "I left her consulting room immediately, insisting to pay for the session, no matter how much it cost!"

"Strange!" murmured Dr. Weichelt. "It seems that Rony received Myra Finch's underwear through the intermediary of a patient... A patient who materialized erotic obsessions, or something like that... It's an older story, from about a year and a half ago... It was even written in the papers! Now Rony and Myra are husband and wife, what's more, it seems that they're even expecting a baby...."

"I swear it wasn't me!" I exclaimed.

"I believe you," the doctor calmed me down, "it's only that it fits too well. As for myself, when something fits too well, only then do I start to doubt ... Doesn't that happen to you, too?"

"Oh yes, and how!" I hurried to acquiesce, delighted that, finally, someone was paying attention to what I believed or what I felt. "Then," I added, "all of your colleagues took down so many notes of everything I said, it's quite likely that Dr. Finch convinced another patient to take her underwear to Rony, I mean to Dr. Kaplan; just as it's equally likely that a wretch like me, having come under Kaplan's spell, to have ended at Dr. Finch's beck and call, and maybe this is just how the whole mess ended up ... like Caragiale says: "We don't refuse anything: Mrs. X to Mrs. Y, Mrs. Y to Mrs. Z," and at the end of the line, there's me, who remains untreated in this whole chain of weaknesses, through which, as I've just realized, the only illness that's being cured is Dr. Kaplan's...."

"You mean Finch," Dr. Weichelt interfered seriously. "Don't be surprised! That was the condition of the marriage: he had to take her name, something which suited him just fine. Actually, she was the man in this whole relationship. What's more, Rony's complete healing took place precisely through the symbolic transgression of gender: accepting her name, Rony became in a way a *woman*, this cured him of the obsession *to have them all*, which it seems to me he confessed to you during the sessions... A transition as simple as possible... and perfectly *curative*, as I, too, demonstrated, among other things, a few years ago in a paper which it wouldn't be a bad idea for you to read! Actually," he added blushing, "with me it was exactly the contrary: I was terribly unhappy as a woman, until I decided to become a man!"

"Dear God, take pity on me!" I told myself and I got out of Dr. Weichelt's office, without bothering to recuperate my medical file, with all the analysis and the priceless notes of my torturers, accompanied by the doctor's voice, seemingly more and more of a soprano, which proposed a treatment, naturally long-term and just as infallible!

Having landed on the street, I closed my eyes, feeling the oh-so-familiar dizziness which now seemed much more reassuring, in spite of the sensation of fainting, suffocation and madness or imminent death. As if on cue, the herds of unicorns started frolicking in the sea, with a loud and unbearable roar, while, almost without realizing it, I was touching myself everywhere, with the hope that somewhere I would find a button, where I could turn down the volume....

X

Thus passed a few more months, during which, when I felt ill, I would try different therapies: I cracked about two hundred eggs in the bathtub, I did a thousand push-ups, I bought myself a cuckoo clock, I ran three times to and from my home all the way to the Greek cleaners *Katharsis*, I lit candles, I counted backwards from one thousand in Romanian, English, German, French, Italian, and Spanish, then I tried Hungarian and Aramaic, rather unsuccessfully; I put on a tux and I conducted the overture to *Master Singers* in front of the mirror until the fatigue almost made me faint, I read the *New York Times* obituaries, imagining to myself that I knew all the deceased, I wrote a story about all of them, then I cried, having grown too fond of their lives, I ate germinated wheat kernels and juniper seeds until I couldn't feel my tongue anymore, I made faces at three cops, I spat from twenty bridges, I took the train to Trenton, I bathed all dressed on Coney Island, I took apart a faucet which worked perfectly and I assembled it again, making it work just as well and having six parts left over, which I put into my pocket, I bought a ticket for the national baseball finals which I tore up at the entrance of the stadium, I read *The Life of John F. Kennedy* in a popularized edition, I got an anti-rabies vaccine, I collected Burmese stamps, I recited verses from Vlahuta[13], imagining how Whitman would have written them, then I did the opposite, I drank five glasses of water, twelve of mango juice mixed with chick peas, I waited for four planes with a

[13] Romanian turn-of-the century minor poet whose picturesque patriotism made him a must for secondary school students

delay of over an hour at *La Guardia* airport, I visited the fire-fighters' museum, I let my nails grow for three weeks, I carried a cane, I went to the public baths....

Well, well! All this until one day when, although I had sworn never to go to the doctors again, my heart gave an uncommon flutter, I found in the usual mail an envelope on which my name was clearly written as the addressee, and as the sender: *Dr. William Hellsty, MD, PhD, MSG* and, well, everything else, consequently—what a diploma-ridden psychiatrist! Inside, a kind letter addressed to *me*, since he had just moved to the neighborhood! What delicate attention, I said to myself—ah! the sacred Hippocratic oath!—plus an invitation to a free session! After all that had passed until then, I found it more than appropriate to pay a visit to this unexpected and possible savior! So I ran quickly to Dr. Hellsty, especially since the address was only about two blocks away from where I live. The waiting, not too long: I'd say, neither too-too much, nor too-too little, but what did it matter? You couldn't resist an invitation like this!

The office—a gem! The room was wallpapered in the warmest colors, relaxing music in the background, diplomas in golden frames hung all around. I must say, when he asked me about the *medical file*, I had to give it to him in a roundabout way: I couldn't just say that I had taken to my heels, and that I had left it in the office of one who, although a man, had previously been a woman... He would have taken me for a lunatic!

"I'm perfectly healthy, Doctor!" I tried to answer as *relaxed* as possible, while I felt by his prying looks that, in all proba-

bility, he suspected exactly the opposite. "I took all the necessary tests, even more than was necessary, they were studied by
colleagues of yours, whose names ... I can't recall for the
moment and ... and who, in conclusion, even said, I don't
remember which one of them it was: *mens sana in corpore sano*!
Not to worry, in this respect ... About the file, I lost it, I mislaid
it somewhere among my papers... you know how it is, with so
many papers, mail, notes, which, sometimes, out of careless-
ness, I can say that even the most careful people, like myself,
for example, now that we mention it: I couldn't find it, exactly,
at the pinch: namely, when I came to see you!"

Dr. Hellsty, a man of about sixty years of age, with serious
glasses, was listening to me rather unbelievingly:

"Hm! *Perfectly healthy*—please allow me to have my
doubts concerning this statement. The more tests you take, the
less of a chance you have to be healthy... It's a logical thing,
after all: pure statistics... That's not what intrigues me. Tell me:
Does it happen to you often to forget names or to misplace
things? And I would furthermore like to know: Do you drink a
lot?"

"Me? Goodness, no!" I exclaimed. "Moderately, I mean so-
so, not more than others, and probably more out of fear! I
mean, to give me courage...."

"That's not good," the doctor said. "You shouldn't drink at
all!"

And he idly opened a notebook: it was clear that he would
begin to take notes.

I hurried to stop him.

"No, please, I beg you! Don't write anything in there: I'll give them all to you immediately: Goldenberg, Lieberman, Reichbar, Kaplan, Finch, Weichelt, and then myself...."

"Ah, are you a *doctor*?" he frowned and removed his glasses.

"Yes," I exclaimed, saved. "That's what it is: I'm a doctor! In a way, I treated each one of them... You know, it's more a question of... a *second opinion*, which implies confidentiality, doesn't it...."

"In this case, colleague, you will pay for the session, it seems only natural! As to confidentiality, have no worry!"

Then he listened to me attentively, while I, describing the symptoms, tried to grease them up with *holistics*, *fragmentarism*, *confused states*, and all the other terms, which I now wielded so well. But I adamantly refused to mention Lissy's spitting from heights, the desensitizing unicorns, the epidermics, the undressing in the subway, Rony's underwear, actually Myra's... confidentiality, after all!

"Look," said Dr. Hellsty after a while. "What you have been describing to me so coherently here can lead me to only one conclusion: you suffer from an illness—before we used to call it *panic syndrome*—neuropsychological disorder which manifests itself very drastically, but which has no life-threatening basis, at least not one that has been proven physiologically. To be more precise, where you are concerned, and taking into consideration, of course, the individualized symptomatology, the diagnosis that would suit you best is the one described by Dr. Lewis Goldenberg in his book that came out recently from the

Hopkins University Press... Look, I even have it here, with his autograph...."

He moved about the room for a while, then he brought out a massive volume, hard-cover, bound in inviting colors. He skimmed through it, then he stopped at a certain page:

"*Moft!*" he exclaimed. "That's what you suffer from! And how well he describes it: you said you knew Lissy, didn't you, with his hermit's air, oblivious to almost everything happening outside. Just look how wonderfully he's put it here! Allow me to read you this sentence: "The seal and motto of our times!" That's exactly how it is. I've had more and more cases in the past years, especially with the massive immigration from other territories, which make their own contribution, don't they, to the nuancing of illnesses which we often register—with so much superficiality!—under generic, flat names. That's what you suffer from, too, dear colleague. The symptoms which you've described to me leave no shadow of a doubt!"

I felt as if I were floating. I didn't want to close my eyes only because of the infernal noise of the quadrupeds bathing in the sea....

"May I take a look at the book?" I asked with a voice that sounded more determined than sure... "I was out of the country for a while, I must have received it by mail, because I have a subscription to the Hopkins University Press....

"How else?" said Dr. Hellsty approvingly. "Please!"

It was as if the book almost burned my fingers. I immediately went to the index: A, B, C... finally C ... I look feverishly: Caan, Cabala, Caby... then, directly, Clitoris ... No sign of

Caragiale. Ah! I have a sinister misgiving! I jump directly to P. Parana, Palimpsest, Paranoia, Paranoid... My eyes follow the lines frantically... Pope, *see Vatican*... At last, *Popa*, my name, I go to the page in question: *healed patient*! Oh! The knavish crook! I was afraid that I would arouse Dr. Hellsty's suspicions.

"Go ahead, go ahead," he encouraged me. "I always do the same thing myself, the index is a wonderful digest of a work!"

I now felt reassured in this respect. Let's see what else is in here... Impossible: I find full passages from *Carnival Matters* and *Mr. Leonida Face to Face With the Reactionaries* reduced to diagnoses and neuropsychic symptomatology....

"*Fandacsie!*" I found myself murmuring....

"Oh, yes! *Fandacsy*, I'm glad you've noticed! Don't you think Lissy is brilliant here? Sounds almost like *Ecstasy*! Who would have thought that this whole process with somebody having an obsessive idea could produce a psychosomatic phenomenon of the intensity of a genuine inner earthquake... Fantastic!"

"The only thing is," I decided to retort, "that we have a fundamental lack here. I see that Schulemberg is cited six times in the index; on the other hand another extremely important doctor, also from the Berlin school, and who, I can say, even invented the concept of *fandacsy* that you admire so much in Lissy's work, is entirely missing... I'm even ashamed that my name is mentioned..."

"On the contrary!" said Dr. Hellsty, "Congratulations to you! Any sort of presence in a book as fundamental as this one is important! As to your colleague, whose side you take, per-

haps out of friendship—which is a wonderful sentiment—
maybe his time hasn't come yet, don't worry about it: you're
young, in a new country, where merit will have its reward sooner or later!"

"He's dead," I murmured, "in Berlin," yet without adding
the year, too, since, in any case, it would have been useless.

"I'm sorry," said the doctor, looking insistently at the clock.
"But merits, if they're truly substantial, will be recognized even
post-mortem ... Going back to your symptoms, as a second
opinion, I can't but confirm the diagnosis of our great colleague, Dr. Goldenberg... And I'm especially pleased to know
that one of his collaborators lives near-by... Good-bye, then,
and don't you worry: Lissy says it clearly, one doesn't die of
moft."

XI

"No, but you don't feel whole either," I added, leaving the
office of the last shrink I would ever consult again. English is
better for explaining this matter: in English it's *ever again*. So
that, in fact, I don't know either what will still be.

As to the crises, I gave up both Goldenberg's pills (what a
crook! And who could have given him all the other tips?) and
landscapes with unicorns bathing in the sea. I'm more content
this way: it's not good to dream of a white horse, says Caragiale
somewhere.

Ion Luca Caragiale (1852-1912) is a richly ironic, deadly humoresque, and hard to translate Romanian prose writer and playwright who is credited with inspiring well-marketed-in-the-West Romanian born writers such as Tristan Tzara (father of Dadaism), Urmuz (a Romanian born and died author of surrealist and absurd texts), and, the most famous of all, of Eugène Ionesco. To the Romanians themselves, Caragiale is a tutelary figure invoked during times of crisis: "had Caragiale lived today..." (he would have written pretty much the same).

Moft (pl. *mofturi*) "trifle." "A face mofturi", literally "to make *moft*s" means "to act spoiled," or "to be picky." Caragiale (see note 2 below) turned *moft* into a very general pseudo-concept usable practically in almost any context of Balkan life. The term is a mixture of fun-making, sarcasm, condescension, and dismissal, and is translatable as *"Trifle!", "Really?", "So what?" "You don't say,"* or *"Bullocks!"* as evidenced in the short dialogue: "She: 'I love you!'; He: 'Moft!'". Caragiale, who also edited a magazine called *Moftul Român* (well, yes, *The Romanian Moft*), sometimes uses *moft* as the utterly absurd universal answer to human, experience, language, existence, death, etc.

Thalassemia: an inherited form of anemia caused by faulty synthesis of hemoglobin (Mediterranean anemia)

A *cyclothymic disorder* is an affective disorder characterized by cyclical mood swings.

I feel enormously and see monstrously is from Caragiale's short story *"Grand Hôtel "Victoria Romậna."*

SPUYTEN DUYVIL

All Spuyten Duyvil titles are available through your local bookseller via
Booksense.com

Distributed to the trade by
Biblio Distribution
a division of NBN
1-800-462-6420
http://bibliodistribution.com

All Spuyten Duyvil authors may be contacted at
authors@spuytenduyvil.net

Author appearance information and background at
http://spuytenduyvil.net